Dead in a Park

Leah Norwood Mystery #2

B. L. Blair

Cover art by Nicole Spence at Cover Shot Creations
http://www.covershotcreations.com

ISBN: 0-9906584-7-3
ISBN-13: 978-0-9906584-7-4

CHAPTER 1

I found the body on February 24. It was mid-morning, and the peaceful sounds of the park were in direct contrast to the scene before me. At first I wasn't sure he was actually dead, but one step closer showed me he was laying perfectly still, head at an odd angle, and face-down in the small creek. He was dressed in what appeared to be a custom-made suit, the white collar of his shirt just showing along the neckline of his jacket and a fedora at his side. I looked at him from head to toe and then stopped. Where in the hell were his shoes?

#

"Harry," I called. "Hurry up. I'm tired of waiting."

I paused a moment but got no response. I was standing by the front door of my apartment in the entryway. Nearby is a small table where I toss mail and keys, and next to the table is a coatrack, which was currently empty as I was already wearing my jacket. I waited a moment longer and then headed down the short hallway. My apartment is not large, but I have two bedrooms, a decent-sized living room, and a small but functional kitchen. The room I use as my office is the smaller of the two bedrooms. It contains my desk, computer, and other miscellaneous stuff. My bedroom is a little larger and has a great window. I stopped in the doorway and sighed.

"Harry, not again."

He was sitting on the floor by the window with a pitiful look on his face. The moment I appeared, he turned his soulful brown eyes to me. Directly in the path between Harry and the door sat a small black bundle of fur.

"Pandora, move. Let Harry by."

The cat rose slowly. She stretched out her front paws and arched her back. She gave Harry and then me a disdainful look, took a couple of dainty steps, and jumped onto the bed. She turned around three times, curled up, and promptly fell asleep.

As soon as the cat was out of the way, Harry bounced over to me in a fit of joy, tail wagging, and body shaking. How a fifty-pound dog could be so terrified of a six-pound cat is still a mystery to me.

Harry and Pandora are recent additions to my household. They both came to me on the same day—my thirty-fifth birthday. One as a gift, the other as a stray. Although I have only had them a short time, I can no longer imagine a life without them in it.

I have finally saved enough money for a down payment on a house and have started the process of searching for a home. One day, I mentioned that I would like to get a pet. My well-meaning friends, Gabe and Olivia Weston, along with their three boys, decided to get me a dog for my birthday. Adopted from a nearby shelter, Harry is a large dog. Not exceptionally so, but he is big. The vet thinks he's some cross between a collie, sheepdog, and some other unknown breed. A light brown color, he has a great deal of fur, hence the name Harry. I didn't name him. That had been Eric, the youngest Weston. He thought the play on words was funny. I didn't have the heart to deny Eric his fun so my hairy dog became Harry.

What my friends hadn't known was that earlier that same day I had found Pandora, shivering, wet, and starving under a bush near my apartment stairway. It was obvious that she had been someone's pet. She was friendly and litter box trained, but she had no collar and no chip to identify an owner. We posted flyers around town and even online; however, no one came forward to claim her. So I ended up with two pets instead of one.

Pandora is also an unknown breed. She's extremely small. I had thought she was still a kitten, but the vet had told me she is about two years old. She's just tiny. Like Harry, she has a lot of fur. She had been too thin when I found her, but a steady diet had been all she needed. Although still small, she is healthy and happy. Especially if she can torture Harry.

I bent down, clipped the dog leash onto Harry's collar, and gave him a quick pat. "You need to assert your authority, Harry. You're the top dog."

He just grinned at me, tongue hanging out of his mouth. Pandora raised her head briefly and glared. I laughed at both of them.

"Ready to go, boy?"

Harry bounded to the front of the apartment, pulling me along behind him. We headed out the door, down the stairwell, and through the apartment complex. The complex where I live has a number of individual buildings, each containing four separate apartments. My building is toward the front, facing Ash Street. The pricier units at the back of the complex only have two apartments in each building and face Reed Hill City Park, which is considered a prime location.

Reed Hill is a large town in north Texas with just over ten thousand residents, but it still manages to retain that small town feel. We are a caring community where most people know each other.

Reed Hill City Park is essentially a mini-Central Park. Much, much smaller than the one in New York but lots of trees and grassy areas for picnics and soaking up the sun. It has walking trails and a bike path. There is even a small creek that runs through it. At one end, there is a large open area with a raised platform that is used as a stage for outdoor performances in the spring and summer. The park isn't large, only about five acres, but it has a lot of amenities. It is surrounded mostly by housing, with my apartment complex at one end and houses along one side and the other end. The fourth side has a business building, a couple of restaurants, and a convenience store.

One of the benefits of owning a dog is the exercise. Harry has a lot of energy so I try to walk him each day. We have a routine. As long as the weather is nice, we walk through the complex, across the street, and take a lap around the park. The whole trip normally takes about thirty minutes.

As we neared the park entrance, a familiar figure jogged toward us. Sean Walters is trying desperately to project the struggling artist persona. He dresses in shabby clothes, keeps odd hours, and drinks a little too much. I'm not fooled. He lives in one of the apartments that face the park and drives a BMW that is less than a year old. I have, however, seen some of his work. He is struggling to produce anything worth viewing.

Harry and I run into Sean two or three times a week as he jogs daily and makes multiple laps around the park. He is typically in the park for over an hour. When he saw us, he slowed down. Sean is a large man, over six feet tall, and around two hundred pounds. He isn't fat, just big.

"Morning, Leah," he said when he reached us. He reached out to give Harry a rub on the head. Harry likes most people, especially those who give him some attention. Sean always takes the time to acknowledge the dog and give him a quick pat.

"Hi, Sean. How was your run?"

"Good. The path is dry so you shouldn't have any problems, but if you get off the path, it's a little muddy. I wasn't paying attention to where I was going, and I wandered off and got my shoes all wet."

He picked up one of his feet to show me. The shoe was caked with mud. It looked like he did more than just wander off the path, but I kept that thought to myself. I had seen Sean coming out of some of the wooded areas of the park in the past. There were several places in the park where you could disappear. I figured he was smoking or taking something illegal and didn't want it in his home. He didn't have a roommate, but I had seen him with an older man whom I assume is his father. Sean is young and still learning how to live on his own. He is sweet but not overly self-confident. I don't think he is into anything too bad, but I keep an eye on him.

"Thanks for the heads-up. I'll try to keep Harry on the path. I would hate to have to give him a bath before I left for work."

Sean laughed easily. I was glad to see it. When we first met, I had a hard time getting two words out of him. He's cute but also incredibly shy around people he doesn't know. He's about fifteen years younger than I am. It had taken me several weeks to get him out of his shell, but now we are casual friends. Although he still struggles to talk to me occasionally, he is comfortable enough to ask advice and talk about more than just the weather.

"Leah, I have some new pieces I'd like to show you. I know you go to work late on Thursdays. Can you come look at them now?"

I hesitated. Sean's sculptures were not very good. I often struggled with something to say that wouldn't hurt his feelings. He noticed my hesitation, and his face fell. I don't think very many people are willing to look at his work.

"Sure," I found myself saying. I had the time, and it wouldn't hurt me to spend a few minutes with him. He grinned, which made me glad I had accepted.

Harry and I followed Sean back to his apartment. He lives in one of the buildings that only has two units with an open hallway between them. The apartments are two stories with large windows and lots of floor space.

As we walked through the door, I checked Harry's paws. They still looked okay, and Sean didn't mind the dog in his home. I had been in Sean's unit before. It is tastefully decorated with a large living space and three bedrooms. Two of the bedrooms were upstairs, including the one Sean used as a studio. You could see the park out the big window on one wall. He once told me it helped inspire him while he was working.

"Here're the new pieces," Sean said, pointing to a table near the back. I walked over and looked at them. They were actually quite good but different than anything I had seen from him before. Sean usually worked in clay. His sculptures were abstract in design and typically average-sized pieces, one to two feet tall. They were meant to be displayed in a home or office on a table or stand. The problem with the pieces was that they had no soul. Abstract art can be beautiful, but Sean's work was forced and unimaginative.

The new sculptures were smaller and made of wood. They were specific designs. He had created a majestic lion with a full mane, a large tree with intricate leaves, and what appeared to be a Viking ship. I studied the ship carefully. It was quite distinctive.

The pieces reminded me of a hand-carved sculpture of a rose that I owned. It had been designed and carved by my great-grandfather's brother, Albert. Sean did not have Albert's talent, but these figures were attractive. For the first time, I could see his artistic ability.

"Sean, these are lovely. I didn't know you worked with wood."

"I don't usually," he said shyly. He took a deep breath and stepped forward. He picked up the ship. "I wanted to try something different. Wood has a different feel so I thought I would try to create something less abstract."

"Well, I like them," I said with a smile. On a nearby table, he had several sheets of paper. I absently walked over and picked one up. Before I had a chance to give it more than a glance, the paper was ripped from my hands. I looked up in surprise.

"Sorry," Sean said, quickly gathering the sheets and slipping them in a folder. "Don't…I don't want you…These are new designs. I'm not ready to share them."

"Okay," I said slowly. I backed away a little. Sean had always been very open in the past, talking to me in excruciating detail about his art. He showed me his process and how he worked; however, I had never seen any sketches or designs. This was out of character.

He walked over to the desk in the corner of the room, opened a drawer, and shoved the folder inside. When he turned back to me, he looked embarrassed and nervous. I could understand the embarrassment but not the nervousness. What did he have to be nervous about?

"Sorry, Leah," he muttered. "Really. Those designs…they're just not something I want anyone to see. I don't mean—"

I raised my hand to stop him. If he didn't want me to look at his designs, I wasn't going to intrude. "No problem, Sean. Don't worry about it. Harry and I need to be going anyway."

At the sound of his name, Harry stood up. I grabbed his leash and headed downstairs. Sean followed and showed me out. He apologized again and thanked me for looking at his art. I made some vague answer and walked away. As the door closed behind me, I shook my head, forcing myself not to turn around and question him. Whatever Sean's problems were—and it was obvious he had plenty—they were not my problems to solve.

CHAPTER 2

The entrance to the park that Harry and I use leads directly onto the main walking trail. There is a bike track that skirts the outer edge of the park, but the path for walkers and joggers is a winding trail that leads into the heart of the park and around the other side before winding back to the entrance. It is an enjoyable walk. I like using the trail as there are several places to stop along the way with benches and water fountains. Harry likes using it as it is shaded with a lot of brush and plants to investigate along the route. An occasional bird, rabbit, or squirrel might appear, much to his delight. As it was still technically winter, there weren't too many around, but I knew that in a few weeks, I would be fighting to keep him on the path.

As we walked along the trail, I noticed a few areas with puddles of water. It had rained steadily for three days at the beginning of the week. The last two days had been full of sunshine and warmer weather. The park path is designed to drain quickly, but I could see the grassy area was still wet. I could also hear the small creek flowing nearby. With all the rain, it was running freely. I smiled at the sound. We needed the rain and listening to the babbling brook was a pleasant way to start the day.

It was about ten in the morning so we didn't see very many other people. Most people jog or walk before or after work. I own and work in a store in downtown Reed Hill. My hours vary somewhat so on the days I open the shop, Harry and I get to the park earlier. On those days, I see more people, but on the days I go in late or am off, we often have the park to ourselves. I could see one lone jogger in the distance, but he soon turned the corner and was out of sight. I used the time to think about my day, the errands I needed to run, and the chores I had to complete. Those thoughts didn't last long. I'm very good at compartmentalizing. My thoughts of late surrounded the home I am hoping to buy. I had contacted a real estate agent, and we were going to start looking at houses.

Walking through the park with Harry is a pleasant but invigorating way to start the day. I was getting used to all the extra exercise, but I have to admit, it took a lot of energy to keep up with him. He was walking sedately by my side when my cell phone rang. It was Olivia. Gabe and Olivia Weston are my two best friends. We had met in college and then went into business together. I spoke with one or the other almost every day.

"Hi, Liv."

"Hi, Leah. Do you have a minute?"

"Sure, what do you need?"

"Something is up with Aaron," she said softly. Aaron is the oldest of the three Weston boys. He is almost eleven and has decided he's old enough to do things on his own with little or no supervision. Gabe and Olivia give him as much freedom as they can while still trying to keep him safe. Reed Hill is a close-knit community, but just like every place else, we have our share of predators. Aaron had listened to all the lectures and promised to follow all the rules. As far as I knew, he has been doing just that.

"What do you mean? Is he okay?" I love her kids and spend as much time with them as I can. The boys and I have a special relationship. I'm still an adult they have to obey, but I'm not a parent or teacher. Because I can, I spoil them. They, in turn, sometimes talk to me about things they don't want to tell their parents.

"Yes, yes. He's fine," Olivia continued. "He's just not talking to me much. He disappears and isn't where he said he was going to be."

"He's lying to you?"

"No. Oh, I don't know. I can't say he's lying exactly. For example, he says he's going to Lawrence's house. If I try to find him, he will have been there at some point, but he and Lawrence decided to go to Steve's house instead. Little things like that. He comes home dirty and won't tell me what he's been doing."

It sounded to me like he was just being a ten-year-old boy, but I don't have kids so I didn't voice that to Olivia. Aaron is rambunctious and loud, but he's extremely responsible. I sometimes think he might be a little too responsible. As the oldest, he often takes care of his younger brothers. He takes that obligation very seriously.

"Liv, I'm sure he's fine. Aaron's a good kid."

"I know. You're right." She didn't sound convinced. I could hear the worry in her voice. Olivia is a no-nonsense drill sergeant. She gets a lot done in a short amount of time, and normally she isn't a worrier.

"Why don't we meet for lunch? We can talk about it some more."

"Yeah, that sounds good. What time?"

"I'm still at the park with Harry. One thirty?"

"Okay. I'll meet you at the store," she replied. "Hey, why are you still at the park? Aren't you usually home by now?"

"Yeah, I got caught by Sean." I went on to tell Olivia about my visit with Sean. She had only met him once. He is so shy around new people that he didn't talk to her much. I was still a little concerned about his odd reaction to my seeing his new designs. Olivia knows me too well. She could tell how I badly wanted to interfere.

"Leah," Olivia said. "Sean's a big boy. He'll be all right."

"I know. I'll see you at lunch."

After disconnecting, I forced my thoughts from Sean and back to Aaron. I couldn't imagine what the kid was doing that had Olivia so worried. I just hoped I could reassure her over lunch.

The thought of lunch made my stomach growl. I had a strawberry bagel waiting for me in my kitchen. Strawberry bagels are my favorite. I love anything strawberry. I love the taste, the look, and even the smell. For years, I had tried to find a fragrance that smelled of strawberries without being sickeningly sweet. I wanted the smell of freshly picked strawberries before they have been turned into jellies or pies. Olivia is a chemist and created a perfume for me that smells of ripe strawberries. Leah's Strawberry Essence is the leading product in the lotion and fragrance shop that I own and run.

Scents and Sensibility is the store that Gabe, Olivia, and I opened almost seven years ago. I run the day-to-day operations of selling and promoting. Olivia designs and develops the lotions and fragrances, and Gabe produces, packages, and ships the product. It works well for me because I enjoy the marketing aspect and working with the public. Scents and Sensibility is located just off the main square in downtown Reed Hill. It's a great location. We have paid off all our loans and are now making a comfortable living, which allows me to dream about buying a house where Harry could have his own backyard.

My real estate agent had two houses lined up for me to view. One on Sunday and the other a few days later. The first house was a duplex near the outskirts of town. I didn't think I wanted to live that far from work, and I had doubts about buying a duplex. However, my agent had convinced me it was a really good deal. She said with my budget, the price of the duplex would give me plenty of money left over to upgrade the house and even remodel it into one home. I thought it was worth viewing.

The other house was more in line with what I had envisioned. It was a small three-bedroom bungalow. The location was not far from where I live today. I had driven by on my way home from work one day, and it looked perfect. I tried to keep an open mind, but I was definitely leaning toward the second one. I was getting excited about the prospect of purchasing a house. I am ready to have a permanent place I can call home.

The next step was finding someone to share it with. I didn't mind living alone. I'm content with my life but hope I won't have to spend all of it by myself. Of course, if I'm going to meet someone, I need to get out more. I haven't dated much in the past few years. Getting my store up and running had taken a lot of my time. That is no longer an excuse. I know it's time to re-enter the dating game. I just can't work up any enthusiasm for it.

Two months earlier, I had two men show an interest in me. It had been surprising. Both the men were true alpha males. I didn't usually attract men like that. I'm what most people would describe as average. Average height, average weight, average looks. I have brown eyes and light brown hair. My skin is naturally tan due to inheriting my Hispanic mother's coloring. I'm not unattractive. I'm just not the sort of woman to turn men's heads. That doesn't bother me at all. My older sister is that type of woman. She is incredibly beautiful. I had seen the toll it took on her. Luckily, she is now happily married to a great guy.

I dated both in high school and college, but most of my boyfriends had been nerdy. Not in a bad way. They had been cute and funny. We had a good time together. But none of them would ever have been described as alpha.

Once again my mind had wandered. I glanced down at Harry. He trotted alongside me, searching the bushes for anything that moved. Harry is still a young dog, not quite a year old. He walks on the leash pretty well but is easily distracted. Usually a quick tug from me brings him back in line, but I had known the day would come when the inevitable would happen. As we neared one of the park benches, I stopped to re-tie my shoe. I must have startled the squirrel because it rushed out from under the bench, ran across the walking path, and ran straight into the wooded area on the other side. My grip on Harry's leash was not very strong, and he shot away from me and after the squirrel before I even knew what had happened.

"Harry," I yelled before I ran after him. When I stepped onto the grass on the side of the path, my feet squished. Looking down, I saw the ground was soft and still muddy in places. Just as Sean had warned me, the ground was still wet. I didn't really have a choice as I could hear Harry barking wildly nearby. It sounded like he was close to the creek. I knew he wouldn't come to me unless I was in his sight line. Consigning my shoes to their fate, I waded into the brush. Luckily, it was still winter so the woods and brush in the park were thinner than they would be in a few weeks. I didn't have to go far before I found my dog.

He was standing near the creek bed, barking ferociously at the dead man on the ground. At first, I wasn't sure he was actually dead, but one step closer showed he was laying perfectly still, head at an odd angle, and face-down in the small creek. He was dressed in what appeared to be a custom-made suit, the white collar of his shirt just showing along the neckline of his jacket and a fedora at his side. The suit reminded me of something from the 1930s with the charcoal color and narrow stripes. I looked at him from head to toe and then stopped.

He was so neatly dressed that I was shocked to see that he wasn't wearing any shoes. His feet were encased in socks, but his shoes were nowhere in sight. And who wears a fedora? What was a well-dressed mobster doing in Reed Hill City Park? I couldn't see much of his face, but he looked like a young man. The clothing and hat seemed totally out of place. Harry ran up to me, and I grabbed his leash. Wrapping it tightly around my hand, I pulled him away from the scene and back out to the walking path. I reached in my pocket for my phone. As I dialed 911, I couldn't help but wonder what the hell happened to his shoes.

CHAPTER 3

"Did you see anyone in the area?" asked Megan Ross. Megan is an officer with the Reed Hill Police Department. She was the first one on the scene, along with her partner, Benjie Bottoms. I had met Megan and Benjie the last time I had found a body. Actually, I had met them when someone broke into my store between the last two times I had found a body.

I don't know Megan well as I had only spoken with her briefly, but she seems competent. She is about my age and very pretty although she tries to hide it behind a severe hairstyle and no makeup. It's probably hard for her to be taken seriously in her line of work. As far as I know, she is the only female on the police force in Reed Hill.

"Not really," I told her in answer to her question. "There was a jogger, male, I think, on the trail in front of us, but he was too far away for me to identify. I did see a friend near the entrance. He was returning to his apartment after his jog."

"What's his name?"

I gave her Sean's details and mentioned I had been to his apartment. Megan started to ask me another question but stopped when something over my shoulder caught her attention. Even without turning, I knew what or, I guess I should say whom, it was. I squared my shoulders and turned around slowly.

Chief of Police Alexander Griggs stalked toward us. There was really no other way to describe the smooth, long strides that ate up space. I hate to admit it, but he took my breath away. He isn't exactly gorgeous or handsome, but there is a power about him that draws the eye. He is about five eleven, with broad shoulders and narrow hips. There isn't an ounce of fat on his lean, hard body. Dark hair cut short in a military style covers his head. His face is attractive in a timeless way, and he has a small indentation on the right side of his mouth that drives me crazy. His eyes are a deep, intense green. I had met Griggs when I found the first body back in December.

For a while, I had been a suspect in that case so naturally I did everything I could to clear my name. Griggs had never thought I was guilty, but they had to check all possible suspects and I was high on the list. We had spent three weeks dancing around each other. He was one of the two men I thought might be interested in me. On Christmas Eve, he had pinned me to the back wall of my shop, kissed me senseless, and told me not to leave town. And that was the last time I had seen him.

"What have we got?" he asked Megan in his deep, smoky voice. He has a great voice.

Megan gave her report, and Griggs turned to me. His eyes narrowed slightly as he studied my face. I tried to keep it blank, but I don't think I was very successful. He smirked and said, "So you found another body?"

The anger shot through me so quickly I almost lashed out. He had ignored me for two months and now thought he could be cute? It wasn't like I went around looking for bodies. Isabel had been in the dumpster behind my store. I had found her when I was taking out the trash. And Anthony Thorpe had been inside his own store. Okay, so I did go looking for him, but I hadn't expected to find him dead. I willed the anger down but couldn't keep the glare off my face.

"Actually," I said in a reasonably calm voice, "Harry found the body."

Griggs frowned in confusion until I pointed at the dog. He looked at Harry and then back at me. "When did you get a dog?"

"Five weeks ago. He was a birthday present from the Westons."

"It was your bir —" He broke off and bent down to rub Harry's head. The traitor wagged his tail and barked happily at Griggs. I didn't say anything.

"You had to name him Harry?" Griggs asked as he stood.

"Eric named him Harry," I replied sharply. Suddenly, Griggs grinned. My heart skipped a beat. He also had a great grin.

"Harry because he's so hairy?" he said.

I couldn't keep back the smile. Griggs had met Eric recently. Olivia had taken the boys to tour the police station. She had told me Griggs had taken the time to speak with each of them. Since then, all three boys referenced the chief whenever they could.

The smile slid off my face as the medical examiner arrived, along with Captain David Reddish. Griggs and Megan moved toward them and then headed off into the woods. Just before he moved out of sight, Griggs turned back to me. "You wait here."

I waited for him to turn his back before I rolled my eyes, but I did obey. With a muddy Harry at my feet, I sat down on the park bench to wait. A small crowd had started to gather along the path. Several police officers had closed off the area with yellow crime-scene tape so no one was getting too near. I was inside the tape wishing I could be an outsider looking in.

My watch showed that it had been over an hour since I had left my apartment. Harry was dirty and wet, I needed a shower, and we both needed food. If I made it into work at all today, I was going to be late. I pulled out my phone and called the shop.

"Scents and Sensibility. May I help you?" Kara's voice came on the line.

"Hi, Kara. It's Leah," I said.

"Hi, Leah. I want a number three with a root beer."

In spite of the situation, I laughed softly. On the days I came in late to work, I often stopped at a local fast-food Mexican restaurant and picked up lunch for everyone. Kara loved their chicken tacos.

"Sorry, Kara, that's not why I'm calling. I may not be in today."

"Oh, okay. Is everything all right?"

"Not really. Are there any customers in the store?"

"No, not right now. It's been slow this morning."

"Can you get Emma on the line as well? That way I can tell both of you at the same time."

Emma Mayfield is my assistant manager. She and Kara work for me full-time. I also have one part-time employee, Myra Dewalt. Between the four of us, we are able to cover all the hours the store is opened. Although the shop isn't very busy during the week except around holidays, I wanted two people working at all times. I'm a firm believer in safety in numbers. Reed Hill does not have a high crime rate, but my employees have the right to feel safe.

When Emma got on the line, I quickly explained the situation. I had expected them both to have a lot of questions, and they did. I answered them as best I could, which wasn't very well as I really didn't know much. After I told them I probably wouldn't come in today, they assured me they could handle the store.

A noise from the crowd caught my attention. Someone had raised their voice to ask a question. There were only about ten people, but they were clustered together near the tape. The police officers spoke with them quietly. I saw two people I knew. They both lived in my apartment complex. I had never seen either one of them in the park before. The police cars must have attracted their attention. Maxine Jackson waved to me. I smiled slightly but stayed seated.

Finding this body didn't affect me as much as the other two. Maybe it was because I didn't think I knew the person. I could only see a little of his face so it wasn't as much of a shock. Also, there was no blood. The other two bodies I found had been shot. I wasn't sure what had killed this man, but the lack of blood made the scene less messy. It looked to me like he might have broken his neck. The ground was slippery and wet. He could have slipped, but I didn't think a fall like that would have killed him.

What would a well-dressed man be doing walking around the wooded area of the park? His clothes seemed old-fashioned as if he was from another time. The suit and hat were more appropriate for someone who lived during the Depression. A young man today would not normally dress like that. And why wouldn't he be wearing shoes? He could have been carrying his shoes to keep them from getting muddy, and then when he slipped, the shoes fell into the creek and floated away. It seemed a little far-fetched, but it might have been possible. I pictured him in my mind and froze. His socks had not been muddy.

If he had removed his own shoes, his socks would have been at least a little muddy, even if he had never taken a step. I looked at my own tennis shoes, which were coated with mud. My mind turned over all that I had seen. The rest of his clothes had been neat, at least from the back. His hands had been under the body. Someone had to have removed his shoes. It was looking more and more like he had been murdered.

Harry had fallen asleep. He woke for a moment but then simply rolled over to his side and fell back asleep. The movement allowed me to see how muddy he had gotten on his stomach and legs. I didn't want to try to clean him up in my apartment bathtub so while I was waiting for Griggs and the others to return, I placed a call to the groomer.

After I made arrangements to bring Harry in, I called Olivia to reschedule our lunch. She had a dozen questions, none of which I could answer. I was still on the phone when the police emerged from the trees. They were followed by the medical examiner and his team carrying the body. Megan Ross and her partner escorted them around the spectators while Griggs and Reddish made their way over to me. I quickly ended my call.

"Who were you talking to?" Griggs asked sharply when he reached me.

"Olivia," I replied. Griggs raised his eyebrows, but there was nothing he could say. He hadn't told me not to talk to anyone. Harry grunted softly as he sat up and greeted Reddish. Griggs looked down and shook his head.

"You didn't know the victim?" he asked when he returned his attention to me.

"I don't think so, but I didn't really see his face." I paused and then asked, "Who was he?"

"We don't know," Griggs replied. "He didn't have any identification, no wallet, no keys, nothing."

"How did he get here?"

"Why do you want to know?"

"Just curious," I said innocently.

Griggs's eyes were full of amusement as he looked at me, and Reddish laughed. They both know all about my curiosity. I love a good mystery. I read a lot of detective novels and try to solve the mystery along with the protagonist. Movies that feature a mystery are my favorite. If a crime makes the news, I take notes and follow along. I fancy myself a sideline detective. That trait may have been what got me almost killed just before Christmas.

"We don't know." Reddish answered my question. "The uniforms didn't find any unaccounted for vehicle."

David Reddish is a hard man to read. He has been a police officer for over thirty years and a detective for the Reed Hill Police Department for eight having moved to town from Dallas. He is a large man, attractive, with broad shoulders and flat stomach. He has skin the color of coffee with a dash of cream, but it is his eyes that tell you he's not someone you want to cross. They are hard and calculating.

I had thought he believed I was guilty of murdering Isabel Meeks back in December. He had grilled me and made me feel guilty; however, over the last two months, I had gotten to know him better. Soft-spoken and always polite, he often stops by my store. He told me it was just to see how I was doing. It hasn't escaped my notice that he only stops in when Myra is also working. They are about the same age—late fifties. Myra went through a nasty divorce a few years back so I'm not sure she's looking for a relationship, but she does seem to enjoy David's company. I keep my mouth shut and watch from the sidelines.

"Was he murdered?" I asked softly.

"Oh, yes. It was murder," Griggs replied.

The last time I found a body it had never occurred to me that the police would consider me a suspect. As a law-abiding citizen, I had just assumed that people knew I was innocent. My experience with the police showed me I was wrong. I looked at both Griggs and Reddish.

"Please tell me you don't think I killed him."

Griggs snorted. "No, we don't think you killed him. He was taller than you, and his neck was broken. No way could you have done that."

"It was fast and neat," Reddish added and then turned to Griggs. "Probably someone with military or combat training."

"Someone who knows how to kill with their hands," Griggs said softly.

I swallowed. Candace had shot and killed two people in December and tried to kill me twice. She had been crazy, her behavior unexpected and unpredictable, which had made the situation scary. This sounded worse. A person who was calm and rational murdering someone with their bare hands was chilling. And I couldn't forget about the weird shoe thing.

"Did you find his shoes?"

"No," Griggs replied, turning toward me.

"Why would someone want his shoes?"

"Who knows? There wasn't much of a struggle, although there were multiple sets of footprints. But all appeared to be made by people wearing shoes." He turned away from me and back toward Reddish. "Between Leah and her dog stomping around, I doubt we'll get any viable footprints."

"Hey," I said indignantly. Both men ignored me.

"Let's keep the area secure anyway," Griggs continued.

"Send a team out to see if they can find anything. Maybe the shoes will show up somewhere else in the park."

"Got it," Reddish replied as he started to walk away. "See you around, Leah."

"Bye, David," I said reluctantly. I didn't want to be alone with Griggs. It was awkward and unpleasant. I'm not exactly sure why he had kissed me and then disappeared from my life, but I wasn't going to ask. I hadn't thought he would be interested in me in the first place. Although not traditionally handsome, Griggs is an extremely attractive and sexy man. After waiting weeks for him to call or come by, I finally chalked it up to a gaffe on his part. Instead of telling me he wasn't interested, he simply disappeared. If I hadn't found this body, I probably would have never seen him again except in passing.

We stood there in silence for a few moments before Griggs said, "You can leave now. Thank you for your patience."

He sounded so formal and polite. I didn't like it. I gathered Harry's leash, pulled him up, and started to walk away. "Well, I guess…I guess I'll see you around."

Griggs stepped back and let me pass. I hadn't gotten very far before I heard him call my name. When I turned around, he was standing in the same spot with an odd look on his face. He rubbed his hand across his head and then gave me a slight smile. "It was good to see you, Leah."

"Uh, yeah, you too," I stuttered before we both turned and walked away.

CHAPTER 4

The next day I arrived at work with a freshly groomed Harry and a brand new pair of tennis shoes. The freshly groomed Harry was courtesy of Marcia at The Pet Groomers; the new tennis shoes were courtesy of Walmart. Harry liked going to the groomers. They fussed over him and gave him a treat. Even a day later, he still looked and smelled good.

I bring Harry to work with me on the days I often stay late. It was a Friday so the chances of my leaving work at six were minuscule. Harry enjoys being with me, and my employees and customers enjoy spoiling him. He typically stays in the back room of the store, and one of us will take him for a walk a couple of times during the day. It makes us all happy. It also keeps Harry from destroying everything in my home. In general, he is well-behaved, but he doesn't like being left alone with Pandora.

Myra arrived a little before ten, and we opened right on time. I was surprised at the flurry of customers but soon realized they were here to gossip. At first, it was other shop employees. Downtown Reed Hill is listed as a historical site, and it has a large square that has a beautiful old courthouse that is now used for community events and business meetings. The streets directly surrounding the square are littered with antique stores, specialty shops, and unique restaurants. Most of the workers in the downtown area know each other. We are our own small community.

After the first flurry of people, we had a slight lull before our regular customers started arriving. Fridays and Saturdays are our busiest days, but with Valentine's Day over and Easter still more than a month away, things should have been slower. I hate to say it, but dead bodies are good for business. People come in to gossip but try to cover that fact by buying something.

The surprise of the day for me was when Sean Walters walked into my store. Sean and I talk occasionally, usually entering or exiting the park, and we run into each other sporadically at Bowman's Deli, the sandwich shop across from the park. However, he had never come into my store. Sean looked around and made a beeline toward me. He was very agitated.

"Sean, are you okay?"

"I need to speak with you."

"Okay."

"Not here," he said looking around. "In private."

With a sigh, I led him to the back storeroom. There is a door between the store itself and the back room and another door from the back room to outside. The back room is part office and part storage. My desk and a couple of chairs are on one side, and the larger side contains shelves that hold our excess inventory.

Sean flopped dramatically into one of the chairs. This was the most animated I had ever seen him. I sat behind my desk and waited.

"You've got to help me," he said with fear in his eyes.

For the first time, I began to believe something was really wrong. I studied him a moment. He seemed genuinely afraid.

"I'll try, but you have to tell me what's wrong."

"The police think I killed that guy in the park!"

"Why would they think that? Did you know him?"

"No! But you told them I was in the park. They knew all

about how long I'm usually there. They said I had plenty of time to kill him and still meet you at the entrance. I know they're going to arrest me."

I squirmed inwardly. I had told the police about Sean's habits. He jogged around the park multiple times and usually stopped for a break at least once. And by break, I mean he disappeared into the trees. Altogether, he probably spent an hour and a half in the park. I shook off my guilt. I wasn't the only regular who knew about Sean's habits.

"If you didn't kill him, the police won't arrest you. They don't have any evidence." I paused and looked at him. "Do they?"

Sean wouldn't look at me at first. He shifted nervously in his seat. His hands grasped the arm of the chair as his eyes wandered around the room. Finally he looked back at me and said gloomily, "Just my shoes. My shoes had mud all over them so they think I was walking around the wooded area."

"Were you?"

Guilt was written all over his face, and he quickly looked away again. I hid a smile. I didn't think Sean was a murderer, but I was pretty sure he was doing something illegal. I had a feeling his agitated state wasn't because he thought the police might arrest him for murder but because they would learn about his drug habit.

"I…sometimes go into the woods for a smoke."

"A smoke?"

"Cigarettes."

Right, cigarettes. "Why in the woods?"

He sighed. "My dad. It's actually his apartment. Because he travels for business and is gone a lot, most people think it's mine. He doesn't know I smoke, and I don't want him to find out so I hide in the woods."

I just stared at him. He wasn't a very good liar. Did he really think I was that gullible? He didn't say anything else; instead, he gave me a fake but innocent looking smile. I wasn't going to get him to admit to doing anything illegal.

"What exactly do you want me to do?"

"You know the police. You worked with them before when that lady was killed. Tell them I didn't do it."

"They aren't going to just take my word for it, Sean." He started to say something. I stopped him with a gesture. "I'll talk to Captain Reddish, but I can't make any promises."

Sean didn't look happy, but what could he say? I wasn't even sure he wasn't involved. I didn't think he was, but a drug deal gone bad might explain the dead man in the park. The Cantono family used to be the drug dealers in Reed Hill. With that avenue cut off, maybe the dead man was one of the new dealers in the area.

"Leah," Sean said as he got up to leave. "You didn't tell the police about the designs you saw, did you?"

"What?" I asked confused, and then remembered the sketches he had grabbed from me. "No. Why?"

"No reason. I just don't want to show them to anyone. I'm not ready."

"Why would the police want to see your designs, Sean?" Something was off about all of this. There was no reason for Sean's sketches to be of any interest to the police.

"They wouldn't. I just…Never mind." He paused and looked at me. "Please don't say anything about them. Chalk it up to artistic weakness. Okay?"

"Okay," I promised reluctantly.

"Thanks, Leah. See you around."

Sean was gone before I could reply. I racked my brain, trying to think of a reason why Sean would want to keep drawings for small sculptures from the police. Thankfully, Olivia arrived for lunch and distracted me. Gabe, Olivia, and I have known each other for over fifteen years. We have a comfortable and unbreakable friendship. After college, Olivia and I followed Gabe back to his hometown. Gabe and Olivia married and have three wonderful, rowdy boys.

We headed next door to Nora's Bakery to eat. Nora's is owned by a husband and wife team who also own the condominiums behind my store. One of the perks of being manager at Nora's is the free apartment. Some people like the perk; others do not. Candace Hager was the manager at Nora's until she went a little crazy and started killing people. The new manager is a practical, blunt woman named Juliet who keeps her distance from the other merchants. However, she is a great baker. Some of the items she has added to the menu are wonderful. I love Nora's food, but Juliet has not yet warmed up to Reed Hill. Thankfully, I don't have to interact with her very often.

"So tell me about the dead man," Olivia said. We were seated at a table toward the front of the bakery. Olivia is my complete opposite in so many ways. It still surprises me that we are such good friends. She is petite, blonde, and cute while I am average, dark, and not cute.

"Not much to tell," I replied. "I didn't see his face so I don't know who it is. Griggs said he didn't have any identification on him."

"You saw Alex?" Olivia asked. Gabe was on the city council that had hired Griggs. Gabe and Olivia often interacted with the police chief at various functions. I know Olivia likes him, but she is a loyal and fierce friend. I had told her about the kiss but had kept my feelings about his lack of interest since then to myself. I didn't want her to feel obligated to defend or support me.

"Yes, I saw him," I said. "He and David are really the only ones who have enough experience to handle a murder investigation."

"That's true. I hadn't realized how inexperienced our police department was until Isabel was killed."

"Inexperienced in murder investigations. They have lots of experience in other areas. Reed Hill just doesn't have an extremely high murder rate."

"Until recently," Olivia quipped.

I laughed softly. "I guess that's true."

"So how involved are you in the murder investigation?"

I had become a little too involved with the last murder investigation for Olivia's comfort. Being a suspect had made me nosier than usual. Finding the bodies had made me feel obligated to find the killer. Olivia had been concerned about my safety.

"I'll have to sign a statement about finding the body, but that should be the end of my involvement. The police should be able to solve this one even without many experienced officers. Looks like the case will be assigned to David unless they have hired a replacement for Hunter. Do you know if they have?"

Raymond Hunter was a former captain with the Reed Hill Police Department. He had been the mastermind behind the drug smuggling ring that had been operating out of Reed Hill for a few years. The FBI recently arrested Hunter and several members of the Cantono family who were the local drug dealers. The two major players, Hunter and Damian Cantono, were both still in jail, but several other members of the Cantono family and a few others involved with the smuggling were out on bail. Since I had helped put them behind bars in the first place, I made sure I always carried my Glock 9mm in my purse. I didn't think any of them would come after me, but I wasn't willing to take that chance.

"Not that I know of," Olivia replied. "Alex said at the last city council meeting that he hoped to have someone hired by the end of the month."

"That's only a few more days. I wonder if he has someone in mind."

"Maybe. I know he interviewed several people."

The conversation turned general, and it didn't take long for it to land on Aaron. It was obvious that Olivia was truly worried.

"Tell me again what's going on with Aaron," I said. I was hoping if she talked about it she would feel better. I had seen Aaron the weekend before and hadn't noticed anything unusual.

"I know I'm blowing this all out of proportion, but he's acting funny."

"Funny how?"

"Secretive, mostly. He doesn't tell me what he's doing

anymore, and he isn't always where he's supposed to be."

"What do you mean?"

Olivia talked for twenty minutes about Aaron's behavior. Apparently the kid had been disappearing when he was supposed to be with his friends. When Olivia asked him about it, he told her she must have missed him or that he had gone to a different friend's house. He had been coming home dirty which wasn't terribly unusual, but his clothes were also torn.

"You know he has two friends on the street. The other parents and I keep an eye on them, but they're always riding their bikes up and down the street and are over at each other's houses. I spoke with Steve's mom, and she said she had thought they were at our house."

"So basically, the boys are all telling their parents that they're at each other's houses but aren't?"

"We can't prove that they aren't. We weren't watching them that closely, and they do go to each other's homes. I don't keep track of exactly when they arrive and leave, and I doubt the other parents do either. It's possible he was traveling from house to house, and I just missed him."

I had to admit that didn't sound like Aaron. He was a responsible kid. Gabe and Olivia tried to be fair in their dealings with the boys. If Olivia couldn't prove that Aaron wasn't where he said he was, she wasn't going to punish him, but she was worried. Now, I was worried too.

"So what are you going to do?"

"I tried following him, but he saw me." She paused and looked at me. Oh no, I knew that look. Olivia is a no-nonsense person, but she also has a devious streak. "I was hoping you might try to find out what he's up to."

There was a pause in the conversation as the possibilities flew through my head. This was a mystery I could sink my teeth into and not get myself into trouble. I grinned at her. She grinned back.

CHAPTER 5

After lunch, I headed back to Scents and Sensibility. We continued to have a steady stream of customers throughout the afternoon. My mind jumped between worrying about Aaron and worrying about Sean. I was pretty sure that whatever Aaron was doing was fairly innocent. How much trouble could ten-year-old boys get into? Sean, on the other hand, was a different story. He had definitely been acting strangely when I was in his apartment. He was hiding something. The whole business with his design sketches was odd.

I was helping a customer decide on a purchase when a hush fell over the store. The sudden silence caught my attention. I looked up to see Marcus Cantono standing in the doorway. Marcus is tall and muscular. His shoulders fill out his shirt nicely, and he has a flat, lean stomach. He is very well built, and drop-dead gorgeous. He has jet-black hair that he wears a little too long and a classically handsome face with startling blue eyes. Although incredibly handsome, he exudes danger. It is in the way he walks, the way he stands, the way he carries himself. I don't think he is even aware of it.

Most of the times I had seen him before, he had been dressed in jeans, a t-shirt, and black leather jacket. But now he was dressed in a business suit that looked like it cost more than

I made in several months. The style was sharp and professional; nevertheless, he still managed to look menacing. It didn't make him any less attractive.

He is part of the Cantono family, but as far as I know, all his businesses are legitimate. When we met, Marcus had taken a liking to me. He told me he had returned to Reed Hill as his mother was in poor health, and he wanted to help her. He had also told me that I didn't have to be afraid of his family. That was the main reason I wasn't worried about any of them coming after me. My gun might be a deterrent, but he was a bigger one.

Marcus is another man who kissed me and then disappeared from my life. He had shown up at my store on New Year's Eve and informed me I was his date for the evening. I didn't have a better offer so I told him to pick me up in two hours at my apartment. I went home and put on my most flirty skirt, and we went out for dinner and dancing. At the stroke of midnight, he kissed me. I still remember the look of disappointment on his face. I had a feeling my face mirrored his.

"Well, damn," he had said. "It looks like we're destined to be just good friends."

Looking at him standing at the front of my store, it was hard for me to believe the kiss had done nothing for me. He was still the best-looking man I have ever seen. Too bad there was no chemistry. A twitch of his mouth indicated that he was trying to hide a smile. He knew the effect he had on people. The women in the room were half afraid and half aroused. When I narrowed my eyes and glared at him, the twitch turned into a full-fledged smile. I shook my head as several women gasped, including the one next to me.

"Emma," I called. "Can you please come help Annie? She wants a box set of Vanilla Vine."

Emma hurried over to me with wide eyes. I gave her a quick smile, pointed at Marcus, and said, "You, come with me."

As Marcus followed me to the back room, the

conversations started up again. I knew his visit would be the main topic of discussion. Harry jumped up the minute we entered the room. He stopped when he saw Marcus, and I waited to see how he would react. We didn't know much about Harry's life before he came to the shelter, but in general, he was a friendly and happy dog. The only two people he had reacted negatively to were both men.

Marcus looked at Harry and smiled widely. "You got a dog?"

I nodded, stunned at Marcus's reaction. I don't know what I had been expecting, but the pure joy on his face was a surprise. Marcus knelt on the floor and held out a hand to Harry. The dog took one sniff and stepped forward eagerly. Marcus took Harry's head in his hands and rubbed briskly. The dog shook with delight.

"I love dogs," Marcus said.

"I would have never guessed," I replied dryly.

Marcus grinned up at me, and my heart skipped a beat. We might not have chemistry when we kissed, but he could still take my breath away. He gave Harry one last pat and then stood.

"How are you?" he asked me.

"Fine. Why are you here?"

"I can't just stop by to visit a friend?"

I raised an eyebrow and cocked my head before asking, "We're friends?"

"I thought we were…hoped we were."

"I haven't seen or heard from you in almost two months."

"You're pissed," he said.

"I'm not pissed," I replied sharply. Okay, so maybe I was a little pissed, but I wasn't going to let him know that. "That doesn't seem friend-like to me, that's all."

"I could say that I haven't seen or heard from you in almost two months, either," he said.

"Yes, but I don't have your phone number or your address."

"Ah," he said. "Then the fault is mine. In my defense, I

have been busy. My first restaurant in the area is scheduled to open in March. I've been working nonstop."

Marcus had been a successful restaurant owner in LA before moving back to Reed Hill. He planned to continue that success here. When we had gone out on New Year's Eve, he had told me about his plans.

"I've seen the ads for Bella's. I'm looking forward to eating there. Now, why are you really here?"

He laughed softly. "I heard you found another body."

"Word sure gets around fast."

"Yes, it does. Are you okay?"

"I'm fine," I replied. "It wasn't as traumatic as the others. No blood and besides, I didn't know him. That probably shouldn't have made it easier, but it did."

"Are you sure you didn't know him?"

Something in his voice made me pause. I trusted Marcus, but I didn't know him that well. Although he seemed to be on the right side of the law, his family was as close to a crime family as we had in Reed Hill. I walked over to my desk to give me a moment to think. I leaned against it and looked at him.

"I didn't see his face so I can't be sure, but I don't think I know him." If I hadn't been watching, I wouldn't have seen the relief that flew across his face. "Why are you so curious?"

For a moment, Marcus looked uncomfortable. He shifted slightly and looked away. Could the Cantonos be involved with this new murder? I didn't want to even think about that. In spite of what I had said earlier, I did consider Marcus a friend.

"It's not curiosity, it's concern," he answered smoothly.

"Well, thanks but there's no need for concern." I walked around to the other side of the desk. When I looked back at him, he was studying me carefully. "What?"

"You're not going to get involved again, are you?"

I huffed out a breath and sat down. "No. Why do you even care about that?"

"Because the last time you found a body, you were run off the road and almost choked to death."

"Candace was crazy. This body has nothing to do with me."

Again, Marcus looked uncomfortable. I started to worry. It was obvious he knew something. "Marcus, what are you not telling me?"

"Nothing," he said quickly and headed for the door. "Keep that dog close to you. What's his name anyway?"

"Harry," I said slowly.

The grin was back. "Harry?"

"I didn't name him," I said with a sigh. "Marcus, what's going on?"

"Nothing," he said again. He walked over to me and gave me a kiss on the forehead. He then picked up a pen and wrote on a piece of paper. "My phone number and address. We are friends, Leah. Call me if you need anything."

I stared at the door after he left wondering what to do. I knew Damian Cantono was still in jail, but the Cantonos had a lot of friends. Drugs were one reason why a well-dressed man in a business suit might be in the wooded area of the park. Drugs in Reed Hill equaled the Cantono family. Marcus had told me he would make sure the "family business" was shut down. For the first time, I wondered if he had lied to me.

I didn't have time to think about it long as we had a sudden influx of customers. It was just after five, and everyone had gotten off of work. Those who couldn't come in to gossip during the day decided to stop by on their way home.

Scents and Sensibility is open from ten a.m. until six p.m. Monday through Saturday. Although we technically close at six, we will help any customers still in the store at that time. Because of the heavy traffic that day, we had late customers and a messy shop. I sent Emma and Kara home, but Myra insisted on staying to help me straighten up and restock.

Myra is my one part-time employee. I recently lost my other part-time employee, and Myra requested those hours. It made me happy as I didn't have to hire anyone new. She still works less than twenty hours a week but is a great asset. A former school teacher who took an early retirement, Myra needed something to get her out of the house and around people. She is tall and thin with auburn hair and a very pretty face.

"I haven't heard your version of what happened yesterday," she said to me as we restocked the shelves.

"There are probably a dozen different versions around by now, aren't there?"

"At least."

I told Myra about Harry finding the body. Myra had been around a good deal when I had been suspected of killing Isabel Meeks. She had come to my defense more than once. Now that she was working more hours, we had gotten to know each other even better, and I considered her a good friend.

"Will David be assigned the case?" she asked when I finished.

I glanced at her briefly. Myra is attracted to Captain Reddish. I know it, she knows it, and he knows it. The problem is she went through a nasty divorce. I don't know exactly what happened with her ex, but Myra is skittish. So far, David has been very patient.

"I think so. There isn't anyone else qualified to handle a true murder investigation." Reed Hill did have murders, but most of them were domestic violence cases or physical fights where the killer was known. "Unless the new captain Griggs hires has a lot of experience, David is basically it."

"He won't be stopping by as often, I guess," she said softly.

I had to turn my head so she wouldn't see my smile. I really needed to see what I could do to get that relationship moving forward. "Oh, I imagine he'll find the time."

"Do you think so?"

It was the fear in her voice that finally clued me in. I put down the box I had been emptying and walked over to her. She gave me a tight smile.

"What is it?" I asked.

Myra carefully placed the last container in place. She took a deep breath and turned to me. "I think you should know my ex is in town."

"Oh," I said slowly. Myra didn't talk about her ex-husband. I had determined the little I knew from offhand comments she made and her attitude whenever marriage was mentioned.

"Yes. I don't like to talk about it, but he's abusive. Or he was in the past. I thought you should know that. I don't think he will show up here, but I'm not sure. I can stay away…"

"No," I said quickly. "If he shows up here, we'll deal with it. We'll sic Harry on him."

Myra smiled slightly. I stepped forward and gave her a hug. "Did he threaten you?"

"No," she said. "That's what was so weird. He just showed up at my doorstep and talked about old times. He didn't ask for money or threaten me in any way."

"When was this?"

"Wednesday night."

"Have you seen him since?" I asked.

"No. I told him to leave me alone. I said that if he came back I would file a restraining order. He just laughed and told me not to worry. He was about to come into a lot of money and would be leaving the state. He just wanted to tell me goodbye."

"Well, maybe he's already gone."

"I hope so, but I have this odd feeling that something's not right," she said.

"Why don't you stay with me for a few days?"

Myra had a small house on a few acres of land just on the outskirts of town. It wasn't isolated, but the houses weren't close together. Her neighbors would probably notice if a strange man was hanging around, but they might be too far away to help.

"No." She straightened her shoulders and a determined look crossed her face. "I will not let him scare me out of my home."

"Myra…"

This time the smile she gave me was real. "I'll just take a page from your book. I have a shotgun, and thanks to you, I know how to use it."

I laughed with her. As a young girl, I discovered a talent for shooting. I participated in shooting competitions in both high school and college. Although I no longer compete, I still shoot at a range regularly. After the murders next door to our shop in December, I had offered to teach any of my employees how to shoot. Both Myra and Kara had taken me up on the offer. The three of us had spent several hours at the shooting range over the last few weeks.

"If you change your mind," I said to Myra, "I have a guest room with your name on it."

It was after seven by the time we left. I worried about Myra on the way home. By the time I reached my apartment, I had decided to contact David and tell him what Myra had said. Maybe he could have some patrol cars drive by her place. Myra would probably be mad at me, but I decided I would rather have her mad than dead. It wasn't much, but it would make me feel better.

CHAPTER 6

After arriving home, I changed into some comfortable clothes before searching the refrigerator for something to eat. Friday nights are typically date nights, but other than my failed date with Marcus on New Year's Eve, I hadn't been on a date in over a year. My Friday nights were usually spent on the couch with a good book and Pandora in my lap.

I ate a grilled cheese sandwich for dinner and was considering strawberry pie for dessert when someone knocked on my door. Assuming it was my neighbor who often needs to borrow something, I opened the door without checking who was on the other side. I regretted it instantly.

Griggs and Reddish were standing at my door. I stepped back automatically which they took as an invitation. Before I knew it, both men were in my living room. Griggs watched me as David greeted Harry. Harry loves David and demands attention every time the captain stops by the store. I glanced at them briefly before returning my attention to Griggs. He stood in a relaxed stance with a blank look on this face. He has the best poker face of anyone I have ever met. I couldn't stop the flutter in my stomach, but I schooled my features into what I hoped was simply a friendly expression.

"This is a surprise," I said. "What are you two doing here?"

"Are you alone?" Griggs asked sharply. I didn't like his attitude so I crossed my arms and glared at him. I saw his lips twitch briefly. He raised his hand as if in apology. "I meant we need to speak with you, but I'd like to keep it confidential as long as possible."

"I'm the only person here. I doubt Harry or Pandora will be spreading any gossip."

"Pandora?" Griggs asked in a perplexed voice.

"Her cat," David supplied, pointing to the black bundle of fur on the couch.

"You have a cat, too?"

"Yes. I have a cat too," I said. "What's the big deal?"

"I was just…no, never mind," Griggs said. "We need to ask you some more questions."

"All right. Have a seat. Does anyone want anything to eat or drink? I was about to have some pie."

"Strawberry pie?" David asked.

"Is there any other kind?" I asked with a grin.

Although I'm not a great cook, I can make a really good strawberry pie. David knows this as he had the opportunity to taste one. When I bake, I usually make two pies and take one to work. The last time was the same day he had stopped by to visit.

He grinned back. "I'd love a piece of pie, but we should probably get on with the questions."

I sighed and nodded before sitting on the couch. Pandora immediately crawled into my lap while Harry settled at my feet. Griggs shook his head at the animals. I'm not sure why he thought my having a dog and cat was so odd, but he seemed preoccupied by it. David sat on the other end of the couch, and Griggs took the chair. He studied me a moment.

"You said you didn't know the victim?"

"I said I didn't think I knew the victim. I couldn't see much of his face so I can't say for sure. Should I know him?"

David pulled a picture from his coat pocket and handed it to me. "This is the man. Do you recognize him?"

I studied the picture a moment. It was a young man with

light brown hair and hazel eyes. As when I had found him, he was dressed in a suit. It looked odd on him as it was similar to the other one. Dark with long, broad lapels and stripes. The picture only showed his upper body, but it appeared to be a double-breasted suit. Very strange attire for such a young man. Both Griggs and Reddish seemed to think I should know him, but I had never seen him before. "No, I don't recognize him. Should I?"

"His name is Donald Collins," Griggs said. "Goes by Donnie."

"No." I shook my head. "I don't know him…wait, my grandmother's maiden name was Collins."

Griggs nodded. "Young Donnie is a distant cousin of yours."

"Really?" I looked back down at the picture. My grandmother had passed away about three years ago. She and I had been very close, but I hadn't met anyone from her side of the family. I didn't see any resemblance between Donnie and anyone in my family, but then I didn't look like anyone in my family either.

"Yes," Griggs continued. "Donnie had been arrested numerous times in New York so when we ran his fingerprints, his record popped. We got his picture off the Internet. I didn't think you would want to see his mugshot. We wouldn't have traced him to you except for the ring."

"What ring?"

David pulled out a small plastic bag with a ring inside. When he held it up, I gasped. "That's my great-grandmother's ring."

My grandmother had left me two items when she died. One was a beautifully carved wooden rose, and the other was an intricately designed ruby ring. Both had been given to her mother, my great-grandmother Rose, on her wedding day. The ring had been designed and made by her husband, Arthur. The rose had been designed and carved by Arthur's twin brother, Albert. They are two of my most prized possessions. The rose was sitting in the curio cabinet across the room, but the ring was in a safe deposit box. Or at least I had thought it was.

"It's a fake," David said. I breathed a sigh of relief, but it was short-lived. David continued, "Donnie was killed with his hands tied in front of him, but it was obvious that his pockets had been searched."

"At first," Griggs said, "we believed that the killer was removing all identifying information—wallet, cell phone, keys. Things like that. But now we think he was searching for something."

"He was searching for this ring," I whispered. It appeared I was going to be involved with this case after all.

"The ring was sewn into the lining of Donnie's suit jacket. He was obviously trying to hide it. We took the ring to Gemstones, and Jose Alvera recognized the design and led us to you."

Gemstones was the only fine jewelry store in Reed Hill. The manager, Jenny, was a friend of mine. Jose was her gemologist. He had appraised the ring for me last year. I wasn't surprised he remembered it. The ring was a very unusual design. It contained a single pear-shaped ruby surrounded by a circle of small diamonds. The unique part was the ruby was mounted on a high profile head with the smaller diamonds on a separate basket head surrounding it. This made the ruby much higher than the diamonds, but it still appeared they were fused into one piece. The designer, my great-grandfather, was also well known—not to most people, but definitely to those in the field. Jose had recognized his work immediately.

"May I?" I asked. David handed me the bag. I held it up and studied the ring. It was an exact duplicate, but looking at the stone, I could tell it was a fake. "How can this be? My great-grandfather, Arthur, designed this ring for his wife. All of his design sketches were lost after his death, and this ring has been in our family since then."

"Looks like somebody found the designs. If Donnie was a descendant of your great-grandfather, maybe someone from that side of the family had the sketches."

"Donnie wasn't a descendant of Arthur's. He only had one

child, my grandmother. He did have a twin brother, but they were estranged. I doubt Arthur gave him the sketches, but I suppose it's possible."

"What can you tell us about this ring?" Griggs asked. "Anything special about it?"

"Not that I know of. Arthur was a fairly well-known jewelry designer in his time. There aren't many pieces of his jewelry still in circulation, but the ones left are fairly well known to jewelry appraisers. Some of them are worth quite a bit of money. My ring, the real one, was appraised for over ten thousand dollars, and the stones are not the highest quality. That ring was an early design and a gift to his wife before Arthur started making real money. It's beautiful and I love it, but I don't think it's worth killing over."

"People have been killed for less than ten thousand dollars," Griggs said.

"True," I said. "But someone would've had to know that the ring was worth that much. I didn't know until I had it appraised."

Griggs and Reddish were silent a moment as I handed the fake ring back to David. I didn't know what the ring could possibly have to do with anything. I loved it, but that was for sentimental reasons. The story my grandmother had told me about her parents was romantic.

"Maybe the ring didn't have anything to do with the murder," David said.

"Maybe," Griggs replied, "but the killer was definitely looking for something. Donnie was worried enough that he hid it."

"Hey," I said quickly. "Is that why the killer took his shoes?"

"Probably. Although what they wanted with them is still a mystery." Griggs paused a moment. "Do you have the ring here?"

"No. It's in a safe deposit box at Reed Hill Bank and Trust."

"Good," Griggs said. "We'll need you to verify it's still

there, and let us know if anyone approaches you about it."

"Okay." The bank was open on Saturday mornings. I could check on it before I went to work. Griggs stood, followed by Reddish. I pushed Pandora off my lap and joined them.

"I heard you might think Sean Walters had something to do with it."

"Where did you hear that?" Griggs asked.

"From Sean. He stopped by the store. He asked me to tell you—the police—that he didn't do it."

Griggs and David both grinned. Their reaction didn't surprise me. It was similar to mine.

"Well, then I guess he didn't do it," David said sardonically.

"Yeah, that's kinda what I said to him. I really think he's just worried that you might catch him doing whatever illegal drugs he's doing in the woods."

"He's doing illegal drugs?" Griggs asked.

I shrugged. "Probably. He claims he's smoking cigarettes because he can't smoke in his apartment."

"Unlikely story."

"I didn't buy it either, but when I left his apartment yesterday morning, he was acting strange."

"Strange how?" Griggs asked.

I shrugged. I didn't want to get Sean in any more trouble, and I couldn't see how his reaction to my seeing his designs had anything to do with Donnie's murder. Sean had asked me not to tell the police about them. I wanted to keep my promise so I didn't answer Griggs's question. "You don't think he's involved, do you?"

David shrugged. "Doubtful, but he was in the park during the timeframe Donnie was killed, and he had obviously been in the woods. His shoes were still caked in mud."

"You'd think if he murdered someone, he would get rid of the evidence."

"You saw him when he came out and followed him to his place. It would have been more suspicious if he had gotten rid of them," Griggs told me. "He's probably telling the truth, but we'll keep an eye on him."

I decided I would keep an eye on him too. I hadn't challenged him about his habits before because it wasn't any of my business, and frankly, I didn't care. But Sean had involved me by asking me to speak to the police so now I felt justified.

"I don't think you're in any danger," Griggs said "but we'll have a patrol car in the area just in case."

That reminded me that I had wanted to talk to David about Myra. I told him about what she had said about her ex-husband. A flash of anger crossed his face. I was glad it wasn't directed at me.

"I was hoping you could arrange for a patrol car to drive by her place."

David glanced at Griggs who nodded. David turned back to me. "I'll take care of it right now."

"Thanks," I said as he walked to the door and headed down the stairs. It wasn't until the door closed behind him that I realized he had left me alone with Griggs.

"I'm surprised Cantono isn't here."

"Marcus?"

"Are you dating some other member of the Cantono family?" he asked sarcastically.

"I wasn't aware I was dating any member of the Cantono family."

A look of surprise crossed his face before he narrowed his eyes and studied me. "You aren't dating Marcus Cantono?"

"Not that it's any business of yours, but no. Why?"

"I saw…" He started to say something and then stopped.

"You saw what?"

"Nothing," he said quickly. "Let me know about the ring."

I nodded in agreement. "I'll check on it in the morning."

Griggs walked over to the door and opened it. When he turned back, his gaze locked on me for a moment and then his eyes roamed down my body to my feet and back up again. He gave me a slow, seductive smile, the indentation in his cheek deepening. My heart started beating faster, and I found it hard to breathe. He always affected me this way, and it drove me crazy. The worst part was he knew it. I gave him a dirty look, but he just laughed softly before saying, "Don't leave town."

CHAPTER 7

The next morning, I dropped Harry off at the store and was standing outside Reed Hill Bank and Trust when they opened their doors. I thought about Griggs's parting remark as I waited for them to open the vault. When I first met Griggs, he had told me not to leave town. I had assumed it was because I was a suspect in his murder investigation. After I had been cleared, he said it a couple of more times including right after he kissed me in the back room of my store. I then decided it was his way of flirting. When I didn't hear from him again, I tried to put the whole thing out of my mind. Now, I didn't know what to think.

"Ms. Norwood." A voice penetrated my musing, and I looked up to see a bank employee standing before me. "Please follow me."

A few minutes later, I was staring at the ring. It looked the same to me. I studied it a moment wondering why a copy of it would be hidden in Donnie's jacket. It was a lovely piece of jewelry, but I couldn't think of a reason why someone would want a copy. I grabbed my phone and called Griggs.

"I have the ring," I told him when he answered. "Is there anything I should look for?"

"No," he replied. "We just wanted to know it wasn't

missing. We're still not sure if it has anything to do with the murder."

"So I should leave the ring here?"

"That's probably best. If someone is actually after the ring, the bank vault's the safest place for it."

My mind wandered back to Donnie. In his picture, he looked young, but Griggs said he had been in trouble with the law several times. He couldn't have been that young unless he had started on his life of crime in elementary school.

"How old was Donnie?"

"Twenty-one. Why?"

"He just looked really young in the picture. Has anyone been notified?"

"We contacted next of kin yesterday," Griggs replied. I could hear him shuffling papers. "An uncle, Russell Collins. Apparently Donnie's father died before he was born, and his mother died when he was fifteen. At that point, he went to live with his grandfather, Stanley Collins who passed away a few months ago. The uncle referred us to Wade Collins who is in Oklahoma City."

"Really? He lives in Oklahoma?" My grandmother had lost contact with that side of her family. We didn't know much about them. Oklahoma City was about a three hour drive north of Reed Hill. If I had family living there, it wouldn't be too far for a visit.

"No, he doesn't live there. He's at a convention. It's closer to Reed Hill than New York City so the uncle asked us to contact him."

"Oh," I said. I was a little disappointed. I had hoped that I might meet someone from that side of the family. My sister, Robin, is interested in genealogy. She had the names of our ancestors but had only followed the direct line. These cousins would have a common ancestor if we went back far enough.

"As far as Mr. Collins knew, Donnie was in New York. They were not very close, but he came by late yesterday to ID the body. He's making arrangements…hold on a sec." Griggs spoke to someone before coming back on the line. "I've got to go. Thanks for letting me know about the ring."

"Sure, uh, bye."

"Leah," Griggs called.

"Yes?"

"Try to stay out of trouble."

He hung up before I could reply. I returned the ring to the safe deposit box before heading to work. Emma and Kara had opened the store, and by the time I arrived, there were several people looking around. Downtown Reed Hill is a popular area. Even during the week, we get a lot of traffic from the wealthy north Dallas region, but weekends are our busiest times. I hurried to the back to check on Harry before returning to the front to help with customers. Myra arrived in time to cover for the lunch breaks, and the rest of the day passed quickly.

Around three, I took a break and went to Gemstones to speak with Jose. Gemstones is located on the square facing Main Street. It is between Patina, the antiques store where the murders in December had taken place, and Thompson's Rare Books. Jenny Sanderson, now Kearney, is the manager. Jenny's husband Trent used to work at Patina and was blackmailed into helping Isabel smuggle drugs through the store. Both Jenny and Trent had been suspects in Isabel's murder. Jenny and I became friends during that time as I helped, or at least tried to help, clear Trent's name.

Griggs had said that Jose Alvera had looked at the fake ring and recognized it as a copy of mine from when he had appraised the real one. I wanted to ask him about the copy. Like most people who work retail, Jose's hours vary, but he is usually there on Saturday.

"Hi, Leah," Jenny said when I walked in.

"Hi, Jenny. How are you?"

"Good. The morning sickness is finally gone."

Jenny was four months pregnant and had been battling morning sickness for most of those four months. I hadn't seen her for over a week, but she did look a lot better. She had that pregnant woman glow.

"That's great. You look wonderful." Jenny is of average

height, has light brown hair, and is very pretty. The baby weight had added a few pounds, but she had been slightly too thin before so I thought it looked good on her.

"Thanks," she said with a slight smile. She glanced around the store and then leaned forward to whisper. "I heard you found another body."

"Yeah, in the park. It turned out to be a relative of mine." Jenny gasped softly. I hurried to reassure her. "He was a distant relative—not anyone I knew, but still…"

"Are you all right?" she asked. When I nodded she continued, "So I guess you want to speak with Jose?"

Surprised, I looked at her. Her face was the usual blank canvas. Jenny is very hard to read, but I have gotten to know her fairly well in the past two months and I could see the humor lurking in her eyes.

"Yes," I said shortly.

The humor moved from her eyes onto her entire face. "I knew you wouldn't be able to resist."

"I just want to ask him what he thought about the ring," I said with a shrug.

Jenny laughed and waved me to the back. Like Scents and Sensibility, Gemstones has a back room. Their actual floor space is smaller than mine as they have a smaller inventory, but their back room is bigger. Like most jewelry stores, they have their items displayed in glass cases, and the excess stored under the cases. The back room has an office for Jenny and a huge safe. There is also a long workbench where Jose has the tools he needs to appraise stones and repair jewelry.

He was sitting at the bench when I walked in. He didn't notice me at first as he was looking through a binocular microscope. I cleared my throat softly to get his attention. He looked up and gave a slight smile when he saw me.

Jose is an odd man. He's in his late twenties and doesn't have much in the way of social skills; however, he's incredibly smart. He works as a gemologist because he loves stones. He has a degree in geology and also works part-time for some big oil company. I only know that because Jenny told me. Jose doesn't say much.

"Hi, Jose. Sorry to interrupt." He didn't say anything so I continued. "I wanted to ask you about the ring that the police had you look at."

His face lit up, and he leaned forward in the chair. "It was the same design as yours."

When Jose had appraised my ring, he had raved about the design. Well, he had said about three sentences, which for him is raving. I wasn't surprised he remembered it.

"Yes. I didn't get to look at it for long, but it looked like an exact duplicate to me."

"It was," he said quickly. "Except for the stone."

"Right, the stone was fake," I said.

"And flat."

"Flat?" I asked.

"Your ruby is cut. There's a slight pattern to the stone, and in the middle, there's a slight ridge. It gives the stone texture and reflects light. The ring with the imitation stone was completely flat. No cut to it."

He sat back in the chair as if exhausted from the effort of speaking. I had never heard him string that many words together at once. I thought about what he said. If the stone didn't match, then whoever made the ring probably never saw the original. They must have been working from the sketch.

When I said as much, Jose leaned forward again. There was a weird look in his eyes. "Do you have them?"

"The sketches?" I took a step back. "No. My family has always believed they were lost or destroyed."

"Too bad." He returned to the microscope.

"Well, uh, thanks for the information." He didn't answer, and things were getting a little creepy so I made a hasty retreat.

Jenny was with a customer. I gave her a quick wave and returned to work. I took a few minutes to write down what Griggs and David had told me the night before and what Jose had said about the ring. Jenny was right. I couldn't resist. My love of mysteries made it hard. Whenever there is a crime in the news, I try to learn as much as I can. I keep a notebook with all the clues. I seldom solve the case before the police, but I do enjoy following along.

Two years ago, we had a rash of burglaries in a part of town that was middle class. Hard-working folks who didn't have a lot of extras. It was perplexing as the only items stolen were articles of female clothing, not undergarments, but dresses and blouses. Only one or two pieces were taken from five different homes over a two week period. I had no idea who or why someone would do such a thing and neither did the police, but it was an intriguing mystery. It turned out to be two young boys. Their grandmother, who was their caretaker, had fallen ill and lost a lot of weight. The boys had wanted to give her a new wardrobe for her birthday.

The last murder in town had been in late January. Jamie Wallace had been found in a ditch on the side of the road, the apparent victim of a hit and run. He had been a vile human being, and it hadn't taken me or the police long to suspect his wife of eighteen years. Bonnie Wallace had finally had all she could take. There had been no witnesses, but she hadn't been able to get the car repaired quickly enough to hide the evidence. She was currently residing in the county jail. I heard she looked happier than she has in years.

About an hour before closing, a man walked in and looked around. The majority of our customers are female so when a male comes in we all take notice. He was a large man, tall and wide, average-looking with light brown hair, and dressed in jeans and a polo shirt. He looked to be around forty years old. His nose was a little too big for his face and his eyes a little too beady. He didn't exactly look dangerous, but he did look unpleasant. I made my way over to him.

"Hi. May I help you?"

He smiled. It changed his whole look. His face transformed from unpleasant to attractive. His eyes danced, and he looked ten years younger. I couldn't help but smile back.

"I hope so," he said. "I'm looking for Leah Norwood."

For a moment, I froze. With Donnie's death fresh on my mind, I wondered why he would be looking for me. I quickly took myself to task. People stopped by the store all the time. I gave him another smile.

"I'm Leah."

"Well, hello cousin," he said, offering his hand. "I'm Wade Collins."

"Oh, wow, hi. I'm so pleased to meet you." I shook his hand, which engulfed mine. He had a strong, firm grip. Remembering Donnie I said, "I'm sorry it's not under better circumstances."

The smile left his face. "Yeah, Donnie had some problems. I didn't know him very well, but he didn't deserve that."

There was little else I could say in response so I invited him to the back for coffee. I was excited to learn a little more about my relatives, and Wade seemed willing to talk.

"I understand you came to Oklahoma City for a convention," I said as I handed Wade a cup of coffee. He was seated in one of the chairs in front of my desk. I sat in the other one.

"Yes, the auto show. I lost my job recently due to downsizing. I love cars and always wanted to attend this show so I decided to come before I got another job. It's hard to take time off when you are a new employee."

I know nothing about cars. Sometimes, I even have to look up the make and model of my own car. Gabe was always trying to teach me the basics, but I had absolutely no interest. I made a polite noise and tried to think of something to say.

"Was Donnie interested in cars?"

"He never said. As I mentioned, we weren't very close. I hadn't seen or spoken to him in almost a month and that was just about our grandfather's estate."

"Is that how we are related, through your grandfather?"

"I think it might have been his father, my great-grandfather, Albert."

"My grandmother told me that her father, Arthur Collins, had a twin brother."

"That was Albert," Wade interjected with a smile. "That makes your grandmother and my grandfather first cousins and us…"

"Somewhat more distant," I said with a laugh before sighing quietly. "Donnie was even more distantly related. Do you have any idea why he was in town?"

Wade shrugged. "Not sure but my father said Donnie mentioned he knew someone in the area."

"Who?"

"Dad didn't know much. Said the last name sounded Italian—something with a C, I think."

I slowly put the cup of coffee on the desk. My heartbeat had sped up, and my hands were shaking. At first, I wasn't sure if it was fear or anger. My hand curled into a fist. Yep, it was anger.

As calmly as possible, I asked Wade, "Could it have been Cantono?"

"I guess. Dad said Donnie just mentioned it in passing when Dad told him that I was coming to Oklahoma City for the auto show. Donnie said he had friends that lived a few hours away."

"Was Donnie involved with drugs?"

"I don't know," Wade replied. "He was mostly a small-time thief. Why?"

The door opened, and Emma walked in. She gave me an apologetic smile. "Sorry, Leah. Nora Gomez is asking for you. I tried to convince her that I could answer her questions, but she insists on speaking with you."

Nora Gomez is the newly elected president of the Downtown Business Association. She got the job because no one else wanted it. The association is very active, and most of the merchants are willing to help out. They just don't want to be in charge. Nora is doing a fine job, but she was driving us crazy with all the changes she wanted to implement.

Wade stood up. "I'll get out of your hair."

"When are you leaving town?" I asked him.

"I'm not sure yet. I need to get back home to my family, but I would like to find out who murdered Donnie. My dad and I were all the family he had. I feel bad that I didn't take a greater interest in his life. My own son is about his age. I owe it to the kid to see that his killer is brought to justice."

A sad look crossed his face. Nodding, I touched his arm in sympathy. When Isabel had been murdered, I had felt responsible—not for her death but for finding the killer. I wanted someone to pay for murdering someone I knew. Even someone I didn't like. I hadn't felt that way about Donnie because I didn't know him, but I understood what Wade was feeling.

"Where are you staying?"

"The Holiday Inn."

"Would you like to come over for dinner? I'd like to learn more about your side of the family."

Wade smiled. "I'd like that too."

"I'm not the best cook in the world, but I can grill a couple of steaks."

"That sounds great."

We made arrangements to meet at seven. I gave Wade my address and phone number before following him to the front of the store. After he left, I spoke with Nora. I answered all her questions and reiterated that Emma was perfectly capable of representing our store. Nora smiled at me while Emma rolled her eyes in the background.

We closed on time, and I headed home to get ready for dinner. It had been a long day, but I was looking forward to getting to know Wade better. Hopefully, he could give me a little more insight into Donnie's life.

CHAPTER 8

While preparing dinner, I thought about what Wade had told me about Donnie having friends in the area. Marcus's odd behavior now made sense. He hadn't lied to me, but he had kept me in the dark. Someone in the Cantono family knew Donnie. I took a moment to place a call to Marcus. My anger at him had returned, and I wanted some answers.

"Hello, Leah." His deep voice came through the phone line.

"Who knew Donnie?"

"What do you mean?"

"Don't lie to me, Marcus!" I said harshly.

There was a short pause on the line before he said, "Ricky."

"Ricky?" The name sounded familiar, but I didn't know the names of everyone in Marcus's family. Other than Marcus, the only one I had ever met was Mike, who was still in high school. And that was not under the best of circumstances. He had been sent to warn me away from investigating Isabel's murder.

"Damian's oldest son. Mike's brother."

"You claim we're friends, and yet you didn't tell me. You came by to discover what I knew, not to see how I was." The anger was quickly turning to hurt. Marcus and I had only one date. I knew our relationship was never going to progress romantically, but I still felt something. It wasn't quite definable, but it was there.

"No," Marcus said quickly. "I came by to discover what you knew *and* to see how you were. Ricky is family, Leah. I'm trying to get him and the others on the right path. Donnie was in town visiting, and he asked Ricky about you. He said the two of you were related. When Ricky told me that, I had planned to question Donnie. Unfortunately, I didn't get to before he was killed."

"You should have told me, Marcus."

"Tell you what? That he had asked about you?" Marcus replied. "That's all I knew. Some kid was staying with my nephew, and asked about you."

"He's dead, Marcus. Don't you think I should've known that someone who was murdered had been asking about me? Looking for me?"

"No. He's dead. We both know he was killed because he was involved with something that he shouldn't have been. You're safer if you're not involved."

He was acting like he wanted to protect me, keep me from getting hurt. I just didn't know if he was sincere. I also didn't know if there was anything that would keep me from being involved, but Marcus didn't know about the ring and I couldn't tell him. He hadn't known that Donnie had probably been waiting for me in the park.

"The police need to know," I said softly. The Cantono family did not contact the police. It was usually the other way around.

"I already spoke with Captain Reddish," Marcus said, surprising me.

"You talked to David?"

"Yes. As soon as I heard Donnie was dead, I contacted him. I told him Donnie had been staying with Ricky and Mike in Mayville. I also told him Donnie had mentioned that he was related to you."

"Oh."

"It may not seem like it, Leah, but I am trying to protect

you. Keep you out of another murder investigation."

I sighed. "Okay, but Marcus, I can take care of myself. I deserved to know what was going on."

Suddenly, he chuckled. The sound caused the butterflies in my stomach to jump. "Yes, that's true. You did pull a gun on me."

"I did not!" I paused a moment. "I pulled it on Mike, sort of."

"Goodnight, Leah," Marcus said, humor coloring his voice. I disconnected the call and went to change clothes with Marcus's laughter echoing in my ears.

My guest arrived on time with a nice bottle of wine. We had a pleasant meal while avoiding the topic of Donnie and his murder. Wade told me about his life in New York. He was married, with a son in his first year of college and a sixteen-year-old daughter. I told him how I came to be in Reed Hill and about my family. After we had eaten, I sent him into the living room while I made us some coffee.

Wade was standing in front of my curio cabinet when I joined him in the living room. The cabinet is taller than I am. It is made of light oak and beveled glass. I have only a few items in the cabinet. On the top shelf was the wooden rose given to me by my grandmother. The other shelves contained a few antique perfume bottles and an elaborate teapot one of my sisters had given me.

"Those are beautiful perfume bottles," he said.

"Thanks. Most of them were gifts, but I bought the blue one when I was in Germany."

"Nice. My wife has a small collection too." He paused and leaned forward. "That rose looks like my great-grandfather's work."

I nodded and handed him his coffee. "Yes. Both he and my great-grandfather made some beautiful things."

"Could I get a closer look?" Wade asked hesitantly.

"Of course," I replied. "Let me get the key."

I only have the cabinet locked to keep Pandora from opening the door. The latch needed repair, but I have never gotten around to it. Pandora had learned to pull it open with her paw. She would crawl in and sleep on the bottom shelf. Locking the door kept it in place. I got the key, unlocked the cabinet, and handed the rose to Wade.

He held it up with a smile. He ran his fingers across the rose petals and looked at it from every angle. The rose is carved out of a single piece of wood. The base is a square so that a rose, in full bloom, sat on top of it. Altogether, it is about six inches high and four inches wide. I love it. The look on Wade's face was one of awe. "Beautiful. The intricacy is amazing. This is obviously one of his early pieces. The later ones were not as elaborate."

"That's too bad because this is gorgeous." Wade handed the rose back, and I replaced it in the cabinet. "Why did he change his style?"

"No idea. My grandfather didn't talk about him much. I've learned more about the family history in the last few months than I did growing up. Do you know why he and Arthur were estranged?"

I grinned. "Because of a woman and a great deal of money."

Wade laughed. "I only heard the part about a great deal of money. It sounds like their stories might have been a little different. Tell me your version of the family tale, and I'll tell you mine."

"Okay." I settled back on the couch with my drink. "When the brothers were young, they lived in a small village in England. They were both craftsmen. Arthur designed and made jewelry, and Albert made wooden sculptures, mostly decorative items like my rose."

"He was a talented man."

"Yes, he was. Anyway, they both fell in love with the same girl—my great-grandmother, Rose. She chose Arthur, and they married. Although disappointed, Albert carved her the rose and gave it to her for a wedding present."

"It was a wedding present?" Wade asked.

"According to my grandmother. Soon after that, the

brothers decided to move to the States. They arrived in New York and setup shop next door to each other. Arthur made a great deal of money in a very short time. His jewelry was sought-after and for a few years, he was one of the most sought after artisans. All of his designs were one of a kind. He never made two pieces of jewelry exactly the same." I paused and took a drink of coffee. "Albert became jealous of Arthur, and they fought. Now here's where things become a little muddy. My grandmother said her father began to fear for his life. He was afraid of his brother. He might have had reason because Arthur was shot. Just before he died, he hid most of his money and a few precious gems somewhere in Manhattan. Only my great-grandmother knew the location. He told her he had placed them somewhere safe. When he died, Rose fled New York and moved to Texas. She changed her name when she later remarried. She never told my grandmother where the money was. All she passed on was a few pieces of Arthur's jewelry and that rose."

"How did you get it?"

"I spent a lot of time with my grandmother when I was young. I loved to listen to her stories, and I had always been fascinated by the rose. It's so beautiful. She left it to me, along with Rose's engagement ring when she passed away three years ago. My sisters got the other jewelry."

"Any idea where Arthur hid his loot?"

"No. We don't know if he put it in a safe deposit box, left it with a friend, or even buried it somewhere. It's a mystery."

"Well," Wade said, setting his cup down on the side table, "the version I heard was a little different."

I smiled as I replied, "I'm not surprised."

"According to my grandfather, who was Albert's oldest son, Arthur refused to give Albert his share of the money and after Arthur died, Rose took off with it. My grandfather remembered Rose. He and your grandmother were about the same age. After Rose disappeared, Albert changed and he refused to discuss the money or Rose ever again. My grandfather was very bitter about the whole thing. He always felt he had been cheated out of his rightful inheritance because Rose took the money that belonged to Albert."

"If she took the money, my grandmother never saw it."

"She didn't take the money," Wade said.

"You seem very sure of that."

"I am. My grandfather died five months ago. He lived in the same house all of his life. It had been Albert's house as well. When we were cleaning it out, we found a box with a letter from Rose and a sketchbook."

"Really?" I asked excitedly. My grandmother had often talked about her father's sketches. She had been nine when he died, but she remembered looking through his books and watching him draw.

Wade nodded. "The letter was dated a month after Rose disappeared. She told Albert that the money was gone, and that she had left the gems where Arthur had hidden them. She said they had caused their family nothing but pain. She begged him to leave them and her alone. With the letter, she sent the sketchbook."

"When Arthur died, his jewelry was in high demand. Those sketches would have been worth a good deal," I said. "He never sold them?"

"No," Wade replied. "As far as I can tell, they're all still there. The letter and the sketchbook were wrapped in an old cloth and stored in a box. The letter was postmarked Dallas, Texas."

We were both silent as I took it all in. When I looked back at Wade, he was watching me. I smiled slightly. "He let her go."

"Maybe he really did love her."

"That's how Donnie got a copy of Rose's ring," I said.

"Yes, although why he wanted that one is still a mystery. There were a lot of sketches—many that had never been made into jewelry. If he was looking to sell a piece, you would think he would have chosen one of those."

"I wonder what's so special about that ring."

Wade shrugged his shoulders. "Probably nothing. I hate to

say it, but Donnie was not the most upstanding citizen. He was probably just planning to sell it; try to pass it off as the original. Do you have the original here?"

"No," I replied. "It's in my safe deposit box."

"That's good. That's the safest place for it."

"I guess." I thought about Donnie for a minute and wondered how he got mixed up with Ricky Cantono. "What else can you tell me about Donnie?"

"Just the basics," Wade replied. "My uncle, Isaac, was an alcoholic. He became involved with a young girl named Joyce. Donnie's mother was only sixteen when she became pregnant. Her family didn't really care as Isaac had her move in with him, and it gave them one less mouth to feed."

Wade went on to tell me about Donnie's life. It was a sad story. Isaac had died from a stroke just a few weeks before Donnie was born. Joyce returned to her family, where she and Donnie lived until she died from cancer when he was fifteen.

"Before she died, Joyce did convince my grandfather to let Donnie move in with him. He had already been arrested several times for petty theft, but he settled down a little after his mother died. Granddad made Donnie finish high school. He even took some classes at a community college. He was a smart kid. Donnie then began to work part-time at a law firm. He started wearing nice suits and talking about becoming a lawyer."

I didn't comment on the suits. In my mind, Donnie was dressed like a 1930s gangster, but if Wade thought they were nice suits, I wasn't going to contradict him. It still seemed an odd way for a twenty-one-year-old to dress.

"I wonder how he met Ricky. Did Donnie ever come to Texas?"

"Not that I know of. I think they met in New York."

Mentally, I made a note to ask Marcus. If Donnie was involved with drugs, he might have been introduced to Ricky. The Cantonos had been planning to expand their operation. Maybe Ricky had been sent to New York to make contacts.

Wade stood. "I should be going. Thanks for dinner, Leah. I

enjoyed getting to know you better, but I feel like we just scratched the surface."

"I know. We have years of catching up to do."

"I'll probably be heading home on Monday. I need to get back to my family. Would you like to have an early dinner tomorrow night? My treat."

"Sure, that sounds great."

We made arrangements to meet at five so that Wade would not have a late night. After he left, I added what I had learned from him and Marcus to my notebook. It wasn't much, and I was as confused as ever. If Donnie was in town for some drug deal with Ricky Cantono, where did the ring fit in? And why was he asking about me?

CHAPTER 9

On Sunday morning, I did laundry and cleaned house. My real estate agent called and told me the duplex we were going to view had sold. I wasn't too disappointed as it wasn't the type of home I wanted. So now my afternoon was free. I told Olivia that I would try to follow Aaron and see what he was doing. She was going to let me know when they got home from church. I also placed a couple of phone calls. The first call was to my sister Robin.

Robin has been researching our family history for the past few years. She mentioned she had learned quite a lot about our father's side of the family and was putting it all together to share with the rest of us. If anyone would know about my great-grandfather, it would be her.

"What's wrong?" she asked in lieu of a greeting.

I chuckled softly. My family had not learned of the attempts on my life until after the fact. Both my parents and my siblings have been a little protective of me since then. Normally, we get together for a week once each year, and periodically, the rest of the year for major events. It was only the beginning of March, and I had already seen my parents twice and both of my sisters once.

Robin is the oldest of my siblings, which made her feel

responsible for the rest of us. She is six years my senior and married to her high school sweetheart. They have a nice house in a suburb of Houston and two teenage daughters. We keep in touch but usually only speak about once a month and never at eight thirty on a Sunday morning.

"Nothing's wrong," I told her. "I just need some information."

"Oh, okay, what's up?"

"What can you tell me about Arthur and Albert Collins?"

"Arthur and Albert…Why? What's going on?"

Quickly, I explained what had happened and about the ring hidden in Donnie's jacket. That was all it took. Robin talked nonstop for the next twenty minutes.

When Arthur and Albert moved to New York, they opened retail stores next to each other to sell their jewelry and wood sculptures respectively. Arthur's jewelry store was a huge success, but Albert's failed within a year. Arthur purchased Albert's store and expanded his own. He hired Albert to work for him as a sales associate.

"According to the records I found," Robin said, "Arthur made a lot of money, but he only paid his brother a nominal amount. Arthur and Rose lived well while Albert struggled to make ends meet."

"It sounds like Arthur wasn't a very nice man."

"It's hard to tell, but there was some bad blood between them. You remember how Grandma Sadie used to say her father said that Albert had threatened to kill him, and there were a few news articles that listed Albert as the prime suspect in the murder. Arthur did hide his gems from his brother as well."

"Hmm." I thought for a minute. "Could they have been worth that much? Enough to kill for?"

"At the time of his death, Arthur's store inventory was supposed to include a dozen exceptionally fine diamonds and one unique, unusually large, fire opal. One newspaper article I read stated it was extremely rare and very valuable. Neither the opal nor the diamonds were ever found. The article speculated they were worth close to one hundred thousand dollars."

"Okay, that's a lot of money. Especially back then."

"I know," said Robin. "In today's economy, they would be worth well over a million dollars."

"If Albert felt cheated out of his part of the money Arthur was making, I guess he might have killed him, but I don't really see it. Wade told me that Albert had Arthur's sketches and a letter from Rose. If he wanted money, he could have sold the sketches or had some other jeweler make some of the designs."

Robin sighed softly before saying wistfully, "I would love to see those designs. Wouldn't it be great to have something our great-grandfather drew?"

I laughed. "We have the actual jewelry he made, Robin. You have the emerald necklace, I have the ruby ring, and Ellen has the diamond earrings. I think we did pretty well."

"I know. I shouldn't be greedy. The jewelry is beautiful, but the sketches seem more personal."

"I'll ask Wade if he would be willing to make a copy and send them to us."

"Great."

We talked a little while longer, just catching up. I added a few more notes in my notebook. I still had no idea why Donnie had been looking for me, but I was determined to find out. My second call was to Marcus, asking him to arrange for me to meet with Ricky. He wasn't too happy about it, but he agreed to bring Ricky to the store to talk to me on Monday. If anyone would know why Donnie had been in Reed Hill, it would be Ricky.

I still had a couple of hours before the Westons would be home from church so I decided to do a little research of my own. First, I found and read the articles that Robin had mentioned.

Although the brothers opened their shops in Manhattan, Arthur and his family lived in Parkerville, New York. My great-grandfather was a prominent member of society in that small town so there was a lot of press about his murder. The stories contained a lot of speculation, including the rumors that

Arthur was killed by a mistress, by a poker buddy, and even his wife. But most of the stories revolved around Albert. The leading theory was that Albert was in debt to the mob and needed money from his brother. When Arthur refused to help him, Albert shot him in the head. The story I heard from my grandmother about Arthur hiding the gems never made the news.

On a whim, I did a quick search for Albert's wooden sculptures. There wasn't much to be found. Albert had never earned the success or recognition that Arthur did. There were one or two references, but I didn't discover much until I hit on a collector's webpage. The collector, Trevor Moore, had a personal website where he displayed pictures of wooden sculptures he had purchased or was wanting to obtain.

He actually owned one of Albert's later works. It was a ten-inch bald eagle. It was lovely but lacked the intricate detail and beauty of my rose. It was obvious that it had been designed as a commercial endeavor; however, the collector loved it. He considered it one of his best pieces. He had posted a statement that he was willing to purchase any item that Albert had designed.

Mr. Moore also had a section on his website for comments. He and another collector had a lengthy conversation about Albert's work. They were both huge fans. The second collector mentioned that Albert had made a number of small jewelry boxes after he had to close his store. The boxes were designed for specific pieces of jewelry that had been designed by Arthur and were included as part of the jewelry sale. Many of the boxes were still in circulation.

Another interesting fact I learned was that one of Albert's pieces was on display at The Center for Art in Wood Museum in Philadelphia. I didn't even know there was a wood sculpture museum, but they have some beautiful pieces. A quick search led me to Albert's item, and I got quite a shock. The piece on display was a Viking ship. It looked very similar to the one I had seen in Sean's apartment.

Suddenly, Sean was no longer looking so innocent. I tried

to picture the other two sculptures. I remembered one was a lion and the other a tree, but I couldn't recall any other details. Could the design sketches Sean had hidden from me have belonged to Albert? Had they been old? I didn't remember the paper being fragile, but the sheets could have been a photocopy. Perhaps Sean had been in the park to meet Donnie to purchase the designs. Like Arthur's, Albert's sketches would be worth a great deal of money to the right person. Sean had money, but he didn't seem the type to want a piece of history.

As I had promised Sean I wouldn't mention the designs to the police, I found myself in a bit of a dilemma. It would have taken Sean weeks to create the sculptures I saw so he must have had the designs for a least that amount of time. He may have been in the park to meet Donnie to make a payment, but he didn't have any papers when I saw him. And I had no concrete proof he had anything to do with Donnie. The problem I had was it was too much of a coincidence that he had created a sculpture that looked a lot like one designed by Donnie's great-grandfather. I needed to talk to Sean. I didn't have a phone number for him so I grabbed Harry and went for a walk.

It only took me a few minutes to arrive at Sean's door. I knocked while glancing around the parking lot, looking for his car. I didn't see it and was about to give up when the door opened. To my surprise, it wasn't Sean. Instead, an older man stood in the doorway with a quizzical look on his face. I gave him my best smile.

"Hi. I'm Leah Norwood. I was looking for Sean. Is he in?"

The man smiled back and shook his head. "No sorry. Sean's gone for the weekend. He went to visit some friends in San Antonio."

"Oh, do you know when he'll be back?"

"Not until Tuesday," he replied. "Is there something I can help you with?"

"No…thanks. Sean recently showed me a couple of his new pieces of artwork, and I wanted to look at them again. They were quite lovely."

I waited, hoping he might invite me in. If I could get another look at the sculptures, I might be able to find out if they were also designs that belonged to Albert. If they did, I would go to the police. If they didn't, then I could stop worrying about them.

Unfortunately, the man didn't let me in. He just gave me another smile and told me he would let Sean know I had stopped by. Disappointed, Harry and I returned to my apartment. Now I didn't know what I should do with this new information.

About an hour later, I received a call from Olivia telling me that they were back from church and sitting down to lunch. The plan was for me to be outside the Westons' house waiting when Aaron went out to play with his friends. Olivia had told me that on Saturdays and Sundays the boys would disappear for hours. They claimed they were just playing outside, running from yard to yard, and playing in the vacant lots nearby. They would reappear from time to time to grab a snack or drink so she knew they were still in the neighborhood.

I ate a quick sandwich and then drove across town. Gabe and Olivia live in a large house in one of the newer subdivisions. They had their home built four years ago. It is a beautiful house but looks a lot like the others in the area. I like their home but personally want something with a little more character. That was why I had my real estate agent looking for older homes in town.

I pulled up in front of a house just down the street from the Westons'. I called Olivia and told her I was in place. She informed me Aaron was in his room, changing his clothes. I sat back and waited.

About five minutes later, Aaron walked out of his house and down the sidewalk. He turned right, heading directly toward me. I ducked down quickly trying to hide. I had thought he would head in the other direction. I peeked over the steering wheel in an attempt to see out the windshield while still remaining hidden.

He turned up the walkway of one of the houses about two

down from his own. Before he got to the entryway, the door opened and a boy about his age walked out. I recognized him as Aaron's best friend, Lawrence. They talked a moment and then walked back to the street. Once again, they turned toward me. They headed straight for the house where I was parked. I cursed softly and sat up. There was no way I could avoid Aaron seeing me. He hesitated and then walked to my car. I rolled down the window and gave him a weak smile.

"Aunt Leah?" he said. "What are you doing here?"

"Hey, Aaron. I…" I tried to come up with an excuse for being in the area. I often stopped by their house so that wouldn't be a surprise to him but sitting in a car five houses away was odd—even for me. "I dropped my phone and pulled over to pick it up."

"Oh, okay. You going to the house?"

"Yes. I wanted to talk to your parents about the store," I threw out. That was plausible. "What are you doing?"

He pointed to his friend. "We're just going to Steve's to play."

"Okay. So what are you going to play?"

"I don't know," he said with a shrug. "Maybe football or ride our bikes."

He was a better liar than I was. He had his story ready. If Olivia hadn't told me that she thought they were up to something sneaky, I would have believed him without hesitation. He gave me a quick smile.

"See you, Aunt Leah."

"Have fun," I replied. I watched them walk up to the door and go in. To make my cover story hold up, I drove down to the Westons' and went inside.

Olivia was surprised to see me. She and Gabe tried not to laugh when I told them what had happened but weren't very successful. We were sitting in their kitchen, eating left over peach cobbler.

"I can't believe he caught you," she said, humor lining her voice.

I kicked her under the table. "You didn't do any better. He

caught you too."

"Yes, but I'm his mother. He's always on the lookout for me."

We talked a little longer. Gabe thought we were making too much of the situation, that Aaron was just being a kid. I secretly agreed with him, but Olivia was genuinely worried. If my snooping around would ease her fears then I was willing to continue, no matter how embarrassing it was for me.

The talk quickly turned to the murder. I told them all about Wade's visit and what I had learned about our ancestors. We threw out several theories as to why Donnie might have had the ring, but nothing stood out. After about an hour, I said my goodbyes. I did drive around the neighborhood looking for Aaron and his friends before I left to get ready for my dinner with Wade. They were nowhere to be seen. What was that kid up to?

CHAPTER 10

Mulling over all I had learned that day, I got dressed for dinner. Aaron and his missing friends would have to wait. There wasn't much I could do until I discovered where they were going. Instead, I concentrated on my family's own mystery. The missing gems from Arthur's store inventory indicated that he did hide them. My grandmother had several pieces of his jewelry that she passed down to her grandchildren. My sisters and I, along with two female cousins, each got a piece, but none of them matched the descriptions of the missing items. If Albert was involved with the mafia, then his motive for murder was stronger than I first believed.

Dinner with Wade was enjoyable. We talked like old friends. I called Robin, and the two of them talked about our ancestors. Wade didn't have much to add to Robin's research, but he was very interested in what she had learned about Albert. She offered to send him everything she had, and in return, he said he would send us copies of the sketches.

Wade also placed a call to his father, Russell, and introduced us. It took us awhile to determine the exact relationship between everyone. After much debating, we decided that Russell and I were second cousins once removed, which made Wade and I third cousins. By that point, I was wishing Robin was still on the line because it was confusing as hell, but we had a good time. I did ask Russell if he had ever heard his grandfather talk about the mob. He said he hadn't, but that a neighbor had once told him about the rumors. It was after Albert had died so Russell never had a chance to ask him about it.

Wade was leaving the next morning so we exchanged contact information and promised to keep in touch. I headed home with a full stomach and buzzing head. So many stories and so many people. I needed to sit down and write out all the connections in order to get them straight in my mind.

When I arrived home, I heard a sad whine near the stairwell. I looked around, trying to identify the noise. There are four units in each stairwell on this side of the apartment complex. My apartment and another were upstairs with two on the ground floor. Both of the doors to the downstairs apartments were behind the stairway. A shadow moved near the back wall, and I heard the whine again. I walked around the stairs and found Harry shivering in the corner.

"Harry! Oh my God." I dropped my purse and rushed forward. He whined again but licked my hand when I reached out for him. I ran my hands over him, looking for any injury.

"What happened, boy? How did you get out?" He yelped when I touched his right leg. I could feel swelling on his paw. "Oh, Harry, what happened?"

He moved closer and leaned against me. I patted him carefully looking for any other injury while my mind whirled. How could he have gotten out? I rose and stepped forward to see if he would follow me. He limped slightly but followed me back to the stairs. I wasn't sure if I should try to get him to climb them. I couldn't carry him, but I needed to check my apartment. I bent down and rubbed his face.

"You stay here, Harry. I'll be right back."

Taking a deep breath, I headed up the stairway. When I reached my door, it was slightly ajar. Had someone broken in or had Harry somehow gotten it open? As I moved closer, I could see that the lock was broken. With a shaky hand, I reached out and pushed the door open. I didn't see anything in the foyer so I stepped inside. From the entryway, I could see down the hall and into the living room. There was shattered glass on the floor in front of my curio cabinet. The hair on the back of my neck stood up, and my heart started pounding.

I stood there staring at it until suddenly it occurred to me that whoever had broken in could still be in the apartment. Frantic, I turned and raced out of the apartment. Halfway down the stairs, I remembered my cat. I stopped, turned back, and took two steps up the stairs before stopping again. I couldn't go back up. It would be stupid and irresponsible. Someone could still be inside. If they hurt me, it wouldn't help Pandora. Breathing heavily and body clenched with tension, I headed back down, praying the whole time that she had found somewhere safe to hide.

Harry waited for me at the bottom of the stairway. I pulled my phone from my purse and coaxed Harry to the car. Once settled inside with the doors locked, I called 911. I watched my apartment, but no one came out and nothing moved in the stairway. The burglar must have left before I had gotten home unless he somehow got out one of the back windows.

Fifteen minutes later, a police car pulled into the parking lot. I had settled Harry in the back seat, and he was sound asleep. As I got out of the car, the officers met me on the sidewalk. The first one to me was Keith Cisneros. Keith and I are friendly. I knew him before he became a police officer, and he had been first on the scene when I had found the body of Isabel Meeks behind my store. It had been Keith's first dead body as well. The experience had created an odd bond between the two of us. Keith now made a point of stopping by the store once a week. He treated me like an older sister. With him was an officer I didn't know.

"Hey, Leah," Keith said when he saw me. "What's going on?"

"Someone broke into my apartment. I don't think they're still there, but I didn't want to look."

"That was smart. You okay?"

I nodded. "Harry hurt his leg. I don't know if he was trying to get away from someone or if they hurt him. I don't know where Pandora is."

My voice broke a little at the end. I had found three bodies in the past few months, but the thought of losing my cat almost brought me to tears. Keith looked a little panicked so I took a deep breath and gave him a slight smile. The other officer stepped forward. He was several years older than Keith, probably about thirty. The threat of my tears didn't faze him.

"I'm Luke Snyder. We'll check out your apartment. Wait here."

I returned to the car to wait and called Gabe and Olivia to tell them what happened. Gabe said he would be over as soon as he could. I told him he didn't have to come, but he insisted. It was a relief to know I wouldn't be alone for long. My hands were still shaking, and I had to work to keep the tears at bay. My poor cat. I hoped she was all right.

It didn't take the officers long to search my place. It wasn't very big. Keith came downstairs and motioned to me. Harry was still asleep so I left him in the car and followed Keith up the stairs.

"Did you find her?" I asked as I stepped through the door. Keith looked at me questioningly. "Pandora."

"Oh, uh, no, sorry, we weren't looking for her."

Quickly, I moved down the hallway to the bedroom calling her name. I looked everywhere. Under the bed, in the closet, behind the chair. Finally, I found her in the bathroom, hiding behind the toilet. It took a few minutes to persuade her to come out. I checked for injuries but didn't find any. Once I knew she was safe, I calmed down. I decided the best thing for her at the moment was to leave her in the bathroom.

As I returned to the living room, I looked around, checking the damage. Both officers were standing near the door, talking to Alexander Griggs. I stopped and waited. It happened every time I saw him. My heartbeat sped up and my mouth went dry. I didn't understand why just looking at the man made my toes curl.

Griggs turned and our eyes locked. His gaze traveled down my body and back up. He searched my face. Whatever he saw must have reassured him because he smiled. He stepped forward, took my arm, and led me over to the couch. I sat down and Griggs took the nearby chair.

"Tell me what happened."

I told Griggs about my dinner with Wade and then coming home to find Harry in the stairwell and my door open. After I finished, he said, "We need you to look around and tell us what's missing."

I rose and started taking inventory. The glass was still on the floor. I stepped over it carefully and looked into the curio cabinet. The top two shelves were empty. The perfume bottles were missing as was the wooden rose. I sighed and started listing the items.

"Five perfume bottles and a carved wooden rose are missing from this cabinet. One of the perfume bottles is worth seven to eight hundred dollars. It's a collectible. The others are worth about fifty to sixty dollars each. They're old but not exceptional. I just liked them. The rose was a one-of-a-kind item, but I don't think it would be worth much on the street. Maybe a good auction house would recognize its significance but the average Joe wouldn't." I looked at the coffee table. "My computer tablet is gone. I left it on the table when I went out. That looks like everything in here."

In the bedroom, I discovered that my jewelry case was missing but nothing else. The extra bedroom where I keep my computer was also untouched.

"It looks like the thief tried to grab things that would be easy to fence," Officer Snyder said.

"Put an alert out to the area pawn shops. Maybe we'll get lucky," Griggs said. "Snyder, you and Cisneros talk to her neighbors. See if they saw or heard anything."

"I don't think that will do you much good," I said.

"Why not?" Griggs looked at me impatiently.

"Well, the guy who lives across the hall left for a business trip this afternoon. He always lets me know when he's going to be out of town. The apartment below me is currently empty, which just leaves Mr. Brooks. He's seventy-eight and hard of hearing. He seldom leaves his apartment."

Griggs clenched his jaw before turning back to the officers. "Check anyway. Then talk to residents in the other buildings. People are always coming and going. Someone might have seen something."

Snyder nodded. He and Keith headed to the door just as Gabe appeared. He walked directly to me and gave me a quick hug. "Are you okay? Did you find Pandora?"

I nodded. "She was hiding in the bathroom. Harry's still in the car."

"Good." He offered his hand to Griggs saying, "Hi, Alex. I'm surprised to see you here."

That confused me for a minute. Every time I had called the police, Griggs had shown up so I hadn't been surprised to see him, but then I realized that the chief of police probably didn't normally respond to burglary calls. Gabe and I both looked at Griggs. It was hard to tell, but I thought he might have been embarrassed. He shrugged once and said, "Need to keep up with the case."

"What case? The robbery just happened." Griggs looked at me and waited. It didn't take me long. "No way. You can't think this has something to do with Donnie's murder?"

"I think we have to consider the possibility. A dead man has an exact replica of your ring sewn into his jacket and four days later someone breaks into your apartment?"

"It could be a coincidence," I said softly. I love a good mystery, but I wasn't sure I wanted to be in the middle of one. I like following along with the story, asking questions, learning things. I didn't want to be the target.

"Could be, but it could also be connected. They did take your jewelry case. My guess is they were looking for the real ring."

"What could anyone else want with that ring? It's important to my family, but I don't see how it could be important to anyone else. Why would they break in to get it?"

"That's what we'll need to find out. I have someone coming to dust for prints. You shouldn't stay here tonight. Or at least not alone."

"She can stay with us," Gabe said. He turned to me. "Why don't you gather what you need for tonight? I'll get Pandora."

Soon after that, I was following Gabe back to his house. The police had dusted for prints, and Griggs had rigged the door shut. Keith had assured me he and Snyder would drive by and keep an eye on my place.

After disposing my personal items and Pandora in the guest room, I headed upstairs to say goodnight to the boys. It was after nine, but Olivia had told me that the boys had been worried about me so she let them stay up until I arrived. I spend a lot of time with the Weston family. Aaron, Billy, and Eric mean as much, if not more, to me than my own nieces and nephews.

Billy and Eric had already commandeered Harry. The three of them were on the floor of Eric's room. Harry loves kids and seemed to have bounced back from his ordeal. He was no longer favoring his leg. Both boys were dressed in their pajamas. Olivia had told me to tell them to go to bed as soon as I had reassured them. I talked to them for a few minutes and managed to get a hug from both of them. Eric asked if Harry could spend the night in his room. I agreed and was rewarded with another hug.

I then moved on to Aaron. I had failed to learn anything about what he was doing this afternoon. Maybe now would be a good time to pump him for information. His door was open so I tapped lightly. He was sitting on the bed, watching a home improvement show on television with the Westons' dog, Fido, lying at his feet. Yes, Eric named him as well.

Normally, Aaron would have been with the other boys playing with Harry. Sitting in his room, watching TV was not normal. I was beginning to believe Olivia really did have something to be concerned about.

"Hey, kiddo," I said as I stepped into the room.

He looked up and gave me a tight grin. "Hi, Aunt Leah.

You okay?"

"I am." I briefly told him what happened. He relaxed and told me he was glad I was all right.

"What are you watching?" I asked him.

"Ben Everett," he answered, pointing toward the television.

Ben Everett is a handyman who has a local cable show. I had never watched it myself, but I had heard Gabe mention it.

"Why?" I asked.

"It's interesting. He shows you how to do all sorts of stuff. Normal stuff around the house. He makes it look easy." He paused. "Maybe I'll do something like that when I grow up."

I sat on the chair next to the bed. He sounded normal. He had never expressed an interest in building or construction before, but kids are always trying new things.

"It's something to think about," I told him. "Even if you don't do it for a living, skills like that are good to have."

"Yeah."

"So what's been going on with you?"

"Nothing."

"You haven't been doing anything special? Anything different?"

"No," he said slowly.

"Anything happening at school or…after school?"

"No."

"You're not doing anything outside that's interesting?"

"Just normal stuff."

My line of questioning was going nowhere. Aaron was looking at me like I was crazy, and I couldn't blame him. I sounded like an idiot.

"Good…Great…Well, I guess you better go to sleep. Tomorrow's a school day. Good night."

"Night," Aaron said.

I made a hasty exit. How pathetic was that? I couldn't even interrogate a ten-year-old. I spent the rest of the night wondering what I thought I was doing, wondering what Aaron was up to, and wondering who broke into my apartment and why.

CHAPTER 11

The next day, I left Pandora in the guest room and took Harry with me to my apartment. I had already contacted maintenance. The apartment manager agreed to have the door repaired and the lock replaced. She told me she thought they could have it done by the end of the day. She would call me once it was fixed.

As there was nothing else for me to do, I headed to work. Usually Emma and I open the store on Mondays, but I had thought I would be late so I had asked Myra to come in early. When I arrived at the store, I saw Myra standing by the back door with a man I didn't know. He was huge. Well over six feet tall and at least two hundred and fifty pounds. He was grasping Myra by the arm in a manner that alarmed me.

Both of them turned to look at me when I pulled into the parking space. As owner, I try to treat all my employees fairly, and I don't expect them to do work that I wouldn't do; however, I do keep one perk for myself and that is the personal parking space directly behind the store.

The man said something to Myra as I quickly got out of the car. Harry was right behind me. As we walked around the car, Harry began to bark. He halted in front of the car and stared at the stranger, barking ferociously. I had to keep a tight grasp on his leash as he pulled against it. Harry had only been with me a few weeks, but he had never reacted to anyone so strongly. There had been a couple of people he wouldn't let near him, but he had never threatened them.

"Harry, stop. Be quiet!"

Harry stopped barking but continued to growl. He leaned against me, and I could feel him trembling. The man glared at Harry and then at me.

"Who are you?" he snarled.

I straighten my back and returned his glare. I slipped my hand casually into my purse and felt for my gun. He hadn't threatened anyone yet, but I didn't like the way he was acting. "Leah Norwood. Who are you?"

He took a step back, shot me a dirty look, and then turned to Myra. "You owe me. I'll be by tonight to collect."

With those ominous words, he walked across the parking lot and disappeared around the building. As he walked away, I noticed a white bandage on his right hand. I turned to Myra who looked a little pale.

"Who was that?" I asked. I had a pretty good idea but wanted confirmation.

"My ex," she said. Her voice shook a little. "I'm sorry, Leah. I didn't think he would come here. I thought he had left town."

"Let's get inside."

I unlocked the back door and shooed Myra in. Harry and I followed closely. I locked the door behind us. Motioning Myra to a chair, I went to the store door and looked out. Emma was at the front, unlocking the door. She saw me and waved. I gave her a quick smile and indicated that we would be out to help her in a minute. She nodded.

When I turned back to look at Myra, she was slumped down in the chair with a dejected look on her face. It broke my heart. Myra is a strong and determined woman. She has a kind and gentle nature, but there is steel under her calm exterior. The look on her face was one I would have never associated with her.

"Tell me what happened." I sat in the chair next to her.

"I was at the back door when he called my name. I guess he followed me from my house. He told me he needed money. When I asked him what happened to the big deal he had going, he said it had hit a glitch. He just needed ten thousand dollars, and then I would never see him again."

"Ten thousand…" I started and then stopped. That was a lot of money.

"Yes," Myra said shortly.

"Why does he think you'll give it to him?" She shifted slightly and looked away. Something was truly wrong. "Myra, I'll help you in any way I can, but you have to tell me what's going on."

"I stayed with Leon until my daughter went to college. I would have never stayed with him if it hadn't been for her. Jill loves her dad. They're very close. He's actually a good father—just a terrible husband."

"Did he…hurt you?" I asked quietly.

"A few times. He didn't beat me, but he would grab my arm or shake me. Left a bruise or two. Mostly though, it was verbal. He would say degrading things, call me names." She took a deep breath. "Anyway, the day after Jill left for college, I moved out. I didn't file for divorce right away as our finances were tied up together, and I wanted to get that all sorted out first. It was odd. He didn't fight it. I actually thought it was going to be okay. For a year, nothing happened. We barely spoke. Then one day he showed up at my door demanding money."

"Did you give it to him?"

"Yes."

"Why?" There was something she was not telling me. The woman I knew wouldn't have given him anything.

"Because he threatened to have me arrested."

Stunned, I sat back in the chair. "Okay, you better explain."

"When I left him, I was angry. So very angry. I…I took something of his. A vintage baseball card."

"Okay but couldn't you argue that as you were married, the

card belonged to both of you?"

"No." Myra shook her head. "It was a gift from his father. It was worth almost a thousand dollars. I pawned it for fifty. I did it for revenge."

I bit my lip to keep from laughing. Not at Myra, she was obviously upset, but because it sounded a lot like something I would do.

"It took him a year to track it down," she continued. "He had the paperwork from the pawn shop showing I had sold it."

"I still don't see how that would have gotten you arrested."

"He could have filed charges. He had friends on the police force. They wouldn't have been able to keep me there, and I wouldn't have gone to jail, but they could have arrested me. I almost dared him to do it, but I was less than a year away from thirty years with the school district. I was so close to being able to retire. If I had been arrested, even for that, they would have fired me. I would've lost everything."

I suddenly understood. He had used the one thing that Myra couldn't afford to lose—her reputation. My anger at the man grew. I began thinking about my own revenge. I didn't know what I could do but Leon threatened Myra, and Harry didn't like him. That was good enough for me.

"He can't get you fired from here. They can't take away your retirement. And no one on the Reed Hill Police Department will arrest you."

"No," Myra replied. "He doesn't know that. He thinks I'm still worried about getting arrested. I'm not. He's not getting any money from me, but he was really angry. I don't know what he might do if I don't give him the money."

"We'll tell David. He'll stop him. You can stay with me until this is over." I paused a moment. "Although my place was broken into last night. I don't know how safe it will be."

Myra looked at me and grinned. It was such a relief to see her smile. She looked better than she had since she sat down. "I don't think anyone will break into your place with us there. The only reason they got in was because you were gone."

"So you'll stay with me? At least for a few days?"

Myra nodded. We stood and she gave me a quick hug. "Thank you, Leah. You're a good friend."

Myra went out to assist Emma, and I started on the weekly schedule. Emma, Kara, and my hours are pretty much the same each week, with Myra coming in to help with lunch and breaks. Most of the time we just use the same schedule, but Emma was taking some time off so I had to adjust a few things. I completed the schedule and placed the weekly order for our products before going to lunch. I also contacted David about Myra's ex-husband coming by the store. After telling him she would be staying with me a few days, he assured me he would have the patrol cars keep an eye out for anyone new around the store or my apartment. We both knew the Reed Hill Police Department couldn't spend all their time watching Myra, but there were enough officers who would be willing to do an extra drive-by or two.

After lunch, we weren't very busy so Myra and I went to her place to get her some clothes and take care of her animals. I didn't feel comfortable letting her go out there alone. Until we knew where Leon was and what he was up to, I was going to stick close.

Myra lives on a few acres of land just outside of town. She has two horses and several barn cats. The cats aren't exactly feral, but they aren't pets. Myra provides them with fresh food and water and a warm place to live, and in return, they keep her barn rodent-free.

On the way back into town, we swung by Gabe and Olivia's to pick up my cat before stopping at the apartment to get my new key and drop off Myra's things along with Pandora. We returned to Scents and Sensibility to find Marcus and his nephew waiting for me. Ricky Cantono had Marcus's coloring but none of his good looks. Like all the Cantono family that I had seen, Ricky had dark hair and a thick build. He was almost as tall as Marcus; however, his face had none of his uncle's attractiveness. His eyes were deep set and angry, his nose just a little too pronounced, and there was a wicked looking scar on his chin.

The two men followed me to the back room. Harry jumped up from his bed and greeted Marcus enthusiastically. He responded in kind. I just shook my head. Marcus projects a tough, bad-ass persona. It was still hard for me to grasp this softer side.

I offered them something to drink. Marcus declined but Ricky asked for a soda. They took the two chairs on one side of my desk and I sat behind it. I was glad to have the barrier between us. The permanent look of scorn on Ricky's face was off-putting.

"So what do you want?" he asked with a snarl.

I glanced at Marcus who leaned back in the chair. His eyes laughed at me. Apparently, I was on my own. I turned back to Ricky.

"How did you know Donnie?"

Ricky shrugged. "Met him in New York when I was there on business."

"What kind of business?"

"Personal business."

"Did you sell him drugs? Did he work for you?"

Ricky sat up and glared at me. "Look, lady, I don't got to tell you nothin'."

I sighed and looked at Marcus. "Why did you agree to bring him if he isn't going to answer my questions?"

"I believe you insisted," Marcus said with a smile.

I shot him a dirty look and tried again. "Ricky, do you know why Donnie came to Reed Hill?"

"Just said he was in town and needed a place to crash. Said he was related to you. Some type of cousin or something. He wanted to know where you lived, worked, stuff like that." Ricky paused and tilted his head toward Marcus. "Told Donnie you were off-limits. That Marcus had guaranteed your safety."

Marcus had told me that I didn't have anything to fear back in December. He had said the family business was closing and that I was safe. I didn't realize he had extended it past his family.

"What did Donnie say to that?" I asked.

"Not much. Said he wasn't looking to hurt you. He just wanted to talk. Seemed like he was curious or something like that. He didn't have much family."

"What about his uncle and cousin? They're family," I said. Ricky just shrugged. "Okay, what else?"

"Not much. I told him I heard you walk that dog of yours in the park most mornings."

"Where did you hear that?" I asked sharply.

"Man, the only thing people do in this town is talk. Ever since you found Isabel dead in that dumpster, people talk about you."

Well, that was creepy, but there wasn't really any response I could make. I had no doubt it was true. Reed Hill was just small enough that the gossip mill was a living thing. I thought for a minute. Maybe Donnie was in the park to meet me. I wasn't sure how I felt about that. I wanted to ask Ricky about the ring, but I couldn't do it directly. Griggs wanted to keep it quiet.

"Did Donnie say why he wanted to talk? Did he have anything for me?"

Ricky's eyes focused in on me, and I felt Marcus's scrutiny. I refused to blink. I held Ricky's gaze and waited. Finally, he shrugged, "Nope. Didn't say nothing to me."

I tried another track. "Did Donnie know Sean Walters?"

He froze for just a moment. It was barely noticeable. He looked at me a moment, eyes narrowed and calculating. I wondered what was going through his head. "Who's Sean Walters?"

He was lying. I knew it. Ricky knew Sean, but he wasn't going to admit it. Ricky was involved in all this somehow, but I had no proof. The bigger question for me was whether Marcus was involved. I was no longer sure I could trust him. I rose from the chair and gave them a fake smile.

"Thanks for coming by."

Ricky rose immediately and walked out the door leaving Marcus behind. He turned and studied me. I just stood still, watching him. I didn't know what to say.

"What are you hiding?" he asked me.

"What is *he* hiding?" I shot back.

"I didn't have to bring him here, Leah. I did it because you asked. We're friends, but Ricky is family."

I nodded. At least I knew where I stood with him. He would protect me as long as it didn't hurt his family. I actually understood. My family was important to me too. Of course, mine weren't criminals.

"He knows something."

"Maybe," Marcus acknowledged, "but he isn't going to tell you or me anything. I'll keep an eye on him."

Marcus walked over to the door and looked out into the store. With his back to me, he said, "I can't protect you if you get involved."

Before I could come up with an answer, he walked across the store floor and out the front door.

CHAPTER 12

I was still staring after him when someone knocked on the back door of the store. When I opened the door, Griggs and Megan Ross were standing outside. I stepped back and let them in. Griggs was dressed in his usual work clothes, a suit and tie. I was surprised to see Megan in a suit as well. Normally, she wore a uniform, but she was dressed in navy blue slacks with a matching jacket. She looked sharp and professional.

Harry looked up from his bed and wagged his tail. He rose slowly and walked over to Griggs who reached down to rub his head. Megan looked at the dog with distrust and took a step back. It was an odd reaction, but I didn't ask her about it. She seemed nervous enough.

"We need to speak with you," Griggs said.

"Okay," I said cautiously looking between the two of them.

"Ross is now the lead on this investigation. I'll be shadowing her as this is her first case."

"Really," I said with a smile. "You got promoted?"

She nodded. "Yes. I made captain."

"That's great. Congratulations."

"Thanks," she responded.

It was nice to know she got promoted. I didn't know how

long she had been with the department, but everything about her projected competence and strength. I thought Megan would do a great job. From what David told me, the captains supervised some of the patrol officers and handled the cases that needed detective work. Reed Hill was not large enough to have separate divisions for homicide, robbery, and so on, but we were big enough to need people who could investigate those types of crimes. David and Raymond Hunter, a former captain who is now in jail awaiting trial, had been handling those duties.

I also thought it would be nice for the police to have a female captain. In certain situations, it might be easier for someone to talk to a woman, especially if that someone was a female victim. I'm sure Griggs had thought all of that through before he promoted Megan.

"So what can I do for you?" I asked.

"We've learned that Donnie was staying with Ricky Cantono."

"I know. I just spoke with him."

"You spoke with Ricky Cantono?" Griggs asked sharply.

"Yes. He and Marcus just left actually."

"They were here? And why were you talking to either one of them?"

He sounded a little angry. I looked at him but only saw a blank wall. "First, Marcus is a friend. I asked him to bring Ricky by so that I could talk to him about Donnie."

"Why did you need to talk to him about Donnie?"

"After I spoke with Wade, I realized that Donnie knew someone in the Cantono family so I called Marcus. He told me that he had already contacted David, but I thought Ricky might open up to me a little more than the police."

Griggs shook his head. "I should've known you would learn about that connection. You didn't tell them about the ring, did you?"

"Noooo," I said slowly.

"Leah, what did you…" Griggs started.

"Excuse me," Megan interrupted.

I glanced at her. I had honestly forgotten she was there. She looked a little put out. Griggs stepped back and motioned for her to take over. Megan shook her head briefly.

"Ms. Norwood," she said in a tight voice. "Please start from the beginning and explain what you talked about with Ricky Cantono."

She sounded very professional and a little peeved. I don't know if it was because I had stepped over a line by speaking with Ricky or if she was upset with Griggs for taking over her interview. I hoped it was Griggs. Megan didn't look like someone I wanted angry with me.

"Wade Collins is my cousin," I began, looking at Megan to see if she was aware of the connection. She nodded slightly. I went on to tell them about meeting Wade and learning about Donnie's connection to the Cantonos. I told them everything I learned, although it wasn't much.

"So you didn't mention the ring?" Megan asked. I shook my head and she continued. "Do you think they knew about it?"

"I don't know," I replied. "They both seemed interested when I asked if Donnie had anything for me, but no one said anything about the ring."

"We still don't know if the ring has anything to do with Donnie's murder, but it seems unlikely that he would go to that much trouble to hide it if it wasn't important. Have you learned anything else about it?"

"Not really." I told them about what Robin had said about Arthur and Albert and the rumors surrounding Arthur's death. I also mentioned what Jose had told me about the fake ring. "But the ruby in my ring was not one of the missing gems. He made that ring and gave it to Rose years before his death."

"It's possible Donnie was looking for the missing gems and thought you might have some knowledge of their whereabouts. Maybe he had the ring made from the sketches to prove he was related."

I shrugged. "The sketches themselves would have been better."

"Didn't you say Wade had the sketches? He didn't seemed to think too much of Donnie. Technically, Wade's father now owns the sketches. They might not have been willing to part with them."

"True," I replied.

"I don't think there's anything else we can learn about that at this time," Griggs said. "We do have some information about the break-in at your apartment."

"Anything good?"

"Not much," Megan stated. "We didn't find any fingerprints that matched anyone with a criminal record. There was one set that we couldn't identify, but the others were yours, Gabe and Olivia Weston, and some children's prints that we're assuming belong to the Weston boys."

When she paused, I nodded. Gabe, Olivia, and the boys were at my apartment fairly often. My prints were on file because of my gun license as were Gabe's. I wasn't sure why Olivia's were on file, but it probably had something to do with her former job as a chemist. The other set of prints were probably Wade's. I told Megan that.

"That would make sense," she said. "We did find a small amount of blood near the curio cabinet. Your thief may have cut himself."

The image of Leon's bandaged hand immediately jumped into my mind. It must have shown on my face because Griggs stepped closer.

"What?"

I told them about Myra's ex-husband showing up at the store this morning, Harry's unusually aggressive reaction to him, and his bandaged hand.

"You heard him threaten Myra?" Griggs asked. When I nodded, he turned to Megan. "That's enough to bring him in. Check to see if he has a record. If so, see if his DNA is on file or at least his blood type."

"If we can match the blood type, we can get a court order for his DNA," Megan added.

Griggs nodded. "If we can verify that the blood found in

Leah's apartment matches his, we'll have our thief."

"That seems like a lot of effort and expense to catch a robber who only stole about three thousand dollars' worth of stuff," I said.

"I still think the robbery and Donnie's murder are connected," Griggs told me. "What's Leon's last name?"

My mind went blank. I had never heard Myra even mention his first name until that morning. They had been married so her last name could still be the same as his, but I doubted it. I was about to tell Griggs that I didn't know when I saw that he wasn't speaking to me but looking behind me. I turned to see Myra and Emma standing in the doorway of the storeroom. A glance at the clock told me it was ten after six. They must have closed up while I was speaking with the police.

"Hollins," Myra said distinctly. "Leon Hollins."

Griggs nodded and Megan scribbled it in her notes. Griggs gave Myra a kind smile. "Anything else you can tell us?"

"His blood type is A positive, and he's trying to blackmail me."

There was a slight color to her cheeks showing her embarrassment. I'm not sure who was more surprised by her statement, Griggs, Megan, or Myra herself. I had told them about Leon's threat but hadn't said anything about why.

"Emma," I said quickly. "Everything closed up on the floor?"

"Yes," she said with a nod. She knew something was going on, and she could tell it was a private matter. Emma is a bit of a mother hen, but she was quick to assess the situation. "We're all locked up and restocked. I'm going home."

I gave her a smile of thanks. Myra would be more comfortable talking to the police without an audience.

"Have a good time on your vacation. We'll see you next week."

After Emma left, I had Myra sit behind the desk. Megan sat across and listened while Griggs stood by the door. It was a smart move on his part. Myra definitely found it easier to talk to Megan. She told them basically the same story she had told me earlier. They asked a few questions but didn't linger long on the past.

"Any idea why he's in town?" Megan asked.

"No," Myra replied. "But this morning he was upset. Whatever he had planned did not pan out."

Megan stood. "I'll send a unit to look for him. If he's been in town for a few days, he has to be staying somewhere."

"The two of you be careful," Griggs added. "Stick together. I doubt he'll try anything with Leah around, but if he's our thief, he could also be our murderer."

Myra swallowed, but I just nodded. I wasn't as convinced as Griggs that the robbery and murder were connected. What could I have that someone would kill for? Still, I hadn't liked the way Leon had been acting toward Myra.

"Myra is going to be staying with me for a few days. If you think it's safe at my apartment?"

"Did they get the door and lock fixed?" At my nod, he continued, "Then it should be fine. The thief either got what he or she wanted or what they wanted wasn't there. Either way, there's no reason for them to come back."

He and Megan left soon after. Myra and I grabbed our things and locked up. I got Myra settled at my place and ordered a pizza. We spent a pleasant evening talking. No one tried to break in, and there was no unusual activity.

Griggs called the next morning to let us know that Leon had been arrested late the night before. He had been staying at the Holiday Inn. The police had been able to get a warrant for his DNA based on his blood type matching the blood found in my apartment. When they went to execute the warrant, Leon refused to cooperate so they arrested him.

They also found one of the perfume bottles in his room. All of the other items were still missing. Griggs said that Leon wasn't talking, but between the perfume bottle and the blood, he was sure they could pin the robbery on him.

Myra was relieved that he was in jail and thought it would be safe for her to return to her house after work that evening. She left for Scents and Sensibility while I took Harry for his walk. Tuesday is usually my day off, but with Emma on vacation, I needed to be at the store to cover lunch breaks. As I was only planning to work a couple of hours, there was no need for Harry to come with me.

The store was empty of customers when I arrived at eleven, but soon people started coming in. Myra went to lunch at eleven thirty followed directly by Kara an hour later. My afternoon plans involved following Aaron. I hoped to see where he was going and what he and his friends were doing each day. But before that, I needed something to eat so I decided to grab a sandwich from Nora's Bakery. When I stepped out of the front door of Scents and Sensibility, a dark blue SUV pulled up to the curb and Griggs stepped out.

"Are you leaving?" he asked me as he shut the door.

"Going to lunch," I said pointing over my shoulder.

He looked behind me at Nora's Bakery and then smiled. My stomach churned. I wasn't sure if it was the smile or hunger. Although I wanted it to be hunger, I'm pretty sure it was the smile.

"May I join you?"

"What?" I asked incredulously.

"Come on," he said taking my arm and leading me next door.

It wasn't until we were standing at the counter that I came out of my stupor. I glanced at him. He was dressed casually in jeans, a buttoned-down shirt, and a light jacket. Neither his gun nor badge were anywhere in sight, but I was sure he had both. He looked relaxed and comfortable.

"You're not working?" I asked him.

He shook his head. "Day off."

When I looked surprised, he laughed softly. "I do take one now and then."

"I know. It's just…"

"Hi, Leah." I turned back to the counter and gave Jake Turner a brief smile. Jake is a college student who works part-time at Nora's. He is used to me coming over to get a bite to eat. He returned my smile. "What can I get for you?"

I ordered the lunch special and a glass of tea. Nora's serves breakfast and lunch but has a limited menu. Their main business is pastries and cakes. Each weekday, they have a lunch special, usually some combination of a sandwich, soup, and salad.

"And a strawberry scone?" Jake asked. He knows me really well, and Nora's strawberry scones were the best I've ever tasted. I get them quite often. I nodded quickly and reached into my pocket for some cash.

Griggs stepped a little in front of me and said, "I'll get it. Why don't you choose a table?"

I started to protest and then shrugged. If he wanted to pay for my lunch, I wasn't going to argue. I had originally planned to pick up my food and leave, but Griggs obviously wanted to talk. The store was mostly empty. Only one table was currently occupied. I chose a table in the corner near the back. It was out of the way so we had some privacy.

Griggs joined me a few minutes later with my meal and drink. He had a cup of coffee and a strawberry scone for himself. I guess he had already eaten lunch.

After we were both settled, he asked, "How are you?"

"Fine." I swallowed a bite of my sandwich. "No one tried to break in last night. With Leon in jail, Myra is planning to return to her house tonight. You think that's okay?"

"Should be. We can hold him for a few days. Eventually, a judge will set bail, but until then, she should be safe."

Griggs broke off a corner of the scone and popped it into his mouth. I watched him a minute wondering what he wanted. He was acting differently, casual, friendly. It was bugging the hell out of me.

"So what did you want to talk about?" I finally asked him.

"Nothing in particular." He paused and looked around. "I thought Tuesdays were your day off."

"Normally, but Emma is on vacation. I came in to cover the lunch breaks. Kara and Myra could have probably handled it alone, but I don't like there to be only one person in the store so I came in for a couple of hours."

"But you're off the rest of the day?" When I nodded, he asked, "What are your plans for the rest of the afternoon?"

Looking slyly around the room, I leaned forward and lowered my voice to a whisper. "I'm planning to trail someone. Dig up some dirt."

His face changed immediately. I had known it would. Griggs is a police officer through and through. If he thought I knew someone was doing something illegal, he would expect me to report it. I didn't say a word while I watched the thoughts flicker briefly across his face before his features settled into a blank stare. I had followed Trent back in December when I was still trying to determine if he had been involved in Isabel's death. Griggs had yelled at me. Well, maybe he didn't yell—just told me I was interfering with the investigation. I had thought he trusted me now not to cause problems, but I wasn't sure.

If I hadn't been watching, I wouldn't have seen the humor dancing in his eyes. When he spoke, his voice was stern and unyielding. "Are you interfering in a police investigation, Ms. Norwood?"

"Would I do that?" I asked innocently.

"Hell, yeah," he said with a laugh. "But I don't think you would have told me about it. So, who is it?"

I huffed out a breath, but couldn't deny his accusation. I shook my head and told him about Aaron. Twenty minutes later, I was in the front seat of his SUV, heading to the Weston house.

CHAPTER 13

"Tell me again why you're here," I stated. We were parked on Willow Avenue a few houses down from Gabe and Olivia's. I made sure we were parked in the opposite direction that Aaron had walked on Sunday. I wasn't going to make that mistake twice.

"Aaron would have recognized your car, just like he did last time you tried to follow him," he replied.

"I wasn't going to use my own car," I said in an exasperated voice. "I was going to borrow Myra's."

Griggs turned to me with a stunned look. "Doesn't Myra drive a vintage Mustang?"

Cars were not my thing. I couldn't have told him what type of car Myra drove. I couldn't have told him what type of car I drove. I did know Myra's car was blue, but that was about it. I had considered Kara's as well, but her car was a small, red, sporty one.

"I guess?"

He shook his head. "You would've been spotted easily. Boys, even ten-year-old boys, love cars. One of them would have noticed you."

"You don't think they'll notice this one?"

"Look around." He pointed to a couple of nearby houses.

One had an extended cab pickup, but the other had a SUV almost identical to the one we were in. The only difference I could see was that it was red instead of blue.

"You own a soccer mom car!"

Griggs threw me a dirty look as I laughed. "The point is we won't stick out. The boys won't look twice at this vehicle. We just have to keep them from seeing us inside."

"Is that why you bought it?" I asked. "Because it blends in?"

"No," he said shortly. His hands tightened on the steering wheel. I had hit a nerve. Griggs and I had spent a good bit of time together, but we hadn't talked about personal things very often. Before I could ask him about it, he asked me, "When can we expect them?"

I glanced at my watch. "Fifteen, twenty minutes, maybe a little longer. Olivia picks up the boys from school at three twenty. She makes Aaron do his homework before he can go out. She said he usually leaves the house around four thirty."

"What does Olivia think is the issue?"

"She's not sure there is an issue. She's just concerned because Aaron isn't telling her what he's doing or where he's going. If I can discover that and let her know it isn't anything dangerous…"

"She can stop worrying. I get it."

We talked cursorily for the next thirty minutes. Griggs asked me about my family and told me a little about his. He has one brother. His parents are divorced but still friendly. They live in Houston where Griggs grew up. He had been with the Houston Police Department before taking the chief of police job in Reed Hill. When I asked him how his parents felt about him moving five hours away, he just shrugged. He had been in town since October but no one had been to visit him during that time, and he had stayed in Reed Hill over the Christmas holiday. I thought there might be more to his relationship with his family than he was telling.

We didn't talk about the murder case although I was tempted to tell him about Sean and his designs. It bothered me that one of his sculptures was so similar to Albert's. I still hadn't gotten a chance to talk to Sean himself, but I wanted to talk about it with someone. Griggs was easier to talk to than I remembered.

It was an odd feeling, sitting in the car with him. It almost felt like a first date. Chatting about little things and learning a bit more about each other. I wanted to ask him about the kiss and why he hadn't contacted me, but I couldn't think of a way to ask without sounding needy. I was still a little angry about it. Rationally, I knew I didn't have a right to be upset. He never made any promises, and one kiss doesn't constitute a relationship. It was just hard to convince myself to let it go.

"There he is," Griggs said.

We watched Aaron head down the driveway of his house and turn right. Griggs pulled the car out and started following. Aaron walked two houses down, just like he had on Sunday. We watched him knock on the door before going in. I told Griggs that the house was where Lawrence lived.

"We wait?" I asked Griggs.

He nodded. A few minutes later, Aaron came back out with two boys, Lawrence and Steve. The three boys walked down the street. They were walking casually, but I had the feeling they were keeping their eyes out for anything unusual. Every now and then, one of them would glance behind him. Between me and Olivia, I think we had them spooked. Griggs was much better at deception than I was. He watched the boys carefully. He had already pulled the car to a stop. He leaned forward to keep them in sight but whenever one of them started to turn around, he leaned back into the shadow of the car. The kids were walking directly down the street so we could see them without driving any closer.

"What are they doing?" Griggs muttered.

I suppressed a grin. I had gotten the Reed Hill chief of police interested in a small time mystery. Suddenly, I had to giggle. Griggs glanced at me, surprised.

"What?"

I didn't reply but looked to where the boys had been just a

moment before. They were nowhere to be seen. I quickly looked around. "Did we lose them?"

"No, they went down the alley." Griggs drove the car forward and stopped across from an alleyway. He opened his door and got out. "They're behind the houses. Let's see what they are up to."

I got out of the car and followed Griggs down the alley. It ended abruptly, and we were faced with grass and trees. Directly behind the houses was undeveloped land. Griggs pointed to the ground. The grass was flat and a small trail had formed. I looked down at my new tennis shoes and sighed. Griggs laughed softly as I followed him down the trail. He was wearing sturdy, thick boots.

It wasn't long before we could hear voices. The area didn't have a lot of trees, but it was well-hidden from the street and houses. We had only taken a few more steps when I saw Aaron and his friends standing in front of a rickety, small structure. It had two completed sides made of wooden slats that were used for fencing. A third side was half finished. There was a tarp draped over the top that served as a roof. The boys were huddled together, talking and gesturing. Griggs pulled me back behind a couple of trees. All three of them were facing away from us, but if they turned around one of them might have seen us.

"We only need a few more slats," Lawrence said, pointing to the half-completed side.

Steve nodded. "There're some over on Washington Avenue. I saw them yesterday."

Griggs took my arm and led me back to the alley. Once we reached the pavement, he stopped. He had a troubled look on his face, but I was just confused.

"They're building a fort or clubhouse," I said relieved. He nodded. "Why didn't he tell Olivia?"

Griggs grinned. "What's the point of having a secret club if it's not secret?"

"Okay, I can understand that. Half the fun of it is the secrecy of the whole thing. At least I can tell Olivia, and she can stop worrying about him."

"There's just one problem."

The concern in his voice stopped me. I looked at him questioningly. "What?"

"Where did they get the materials?" Griggs asked.

"What do you mean?"

"The fence slats look new, and that tarp is in pretty good shape. I don't know about you, but when I was ten, I didn't have enough money to buy things like that."

"You think they stole it," I said as a ball of lead formed in my stomach. There was a new section of housing being built nearby. Lots of new houses with fences. "Of course they didn't buy the stuff. No way could they've gotten the slats home without anyone noticing. That's what Steve meant when he said there were some slats over on Washington."

"How do you want to handle it?"

"We have to tell Gabe and Olivia."

I turned and walked back down the alley followed closely by Griggs. An hour later, we were sitting in the Westons' living room when Aaron came home. Gabe and Olivia had asked Griggs to stay as they thought it would scare Aaron more if the police were present.

The meeting with Aaron went as badly as I thought it would. He was angry and sorry. Angry that I had spied on him. Sorry that he got caught. It wasn't until Griggs brought up the stolen materials and compared him to the thief who had taken my things that Aaron broke. I could tell he hadn't thought that taking fence slats was the same thing.

"They were throwing them away," he said tearfully. "After they finished the fence, they put the broken or extra slats out by the dumpsters."

"That may be," Gabe said. "But you didn't have permission to take them. Do you know for sure they weren't going to come back and use the leftover items?"

Aaron shook his head slowly. Gabe frowned but didn't belabor the point. Instead, he sent Aaron to his room, and Griggs and I made our getaway. Back in the car, I leaned my head back on the seat.

"I think I need to find a way to curb my curiosity. I didn't like solving that mystery."

"Sometimes not knowing is better."

"Aaron hates me," I said despondently.

"No, he doesn't," Griggs replied. "He'll be angry for a few days, but he'll forgive you."

"Maybe."

"Do you have your gun?"

The abrupt change of conversation startled me. The question came out of nowhere, and I wasn't sure how to respond. I glanced briefly at my purse where my Glock was securely residing. I had to special order the purse, but the gun fit into the embedded gun holster perfectly. I had started carrying it with me again when I had been threatened by the Cantono family. Recently, I had considered returning it to my safe. Griggs knew I had a concealed handgun license, but I wasn't sure how he felt about me running around town with a gun in my purse.

"Leah," Griggs prompted. "Do you have your gun with you?"

"Why?"

"You do make things difficult," he said with a sigh. "I've heard all about your excellent shooting skills. I thought we could go by the range, and you could prove it."

My shoulders relaxed and I grinned. Shooting was one area I had no worries about. I could out shoot just about anyone. Griggs or some other law enforcement or military personnel might be better, but when it came to target shooting, few could best me.

"I don't have to prove anything," I said cockily.

Griggs laughed. "Okay, how about we just go have fun?"

That sounded like a date to me. Maybe he was toying with me, but I didn't think so. I took a moment to get my heart back under control and then shrugged nonchalantly. "Sure."

Reed Hill has one indoor shooting range. It is a fairly standard range with twelve shooting lanes that have a motorized target system. I have used far worse ranges. I have also been in some pretty fancy places. I expected Griggs to take me there. Instead, he drove to the police station.

After parking at the back, he led me inside. "We have an indoor range in the basement. It's better than the Reed Hill Gun Club although smaller. I thought you might like to try it."

We headed down the stairs to the locked door with a keypad. Griggs entered the code, opened the door, and motioned me in. When I stepped inside, I saw that there was another door with a manned desk behind a glass window.

The man sitting at the desk looked up when we walked in. He stood when he saw us. He was a medium-sized man, but there was something about him that made you pause. Thick shoulders and a tough face. I gave him a nervous smile. Griggs walked around me to the window.

"Hey, Mitchell. We need two lanes." Griggs turned back to me. "Mitchell needs to register your gun."

I nodded and pulled out the Glock. I handed it, along with my driver's license, over without a word. Mitchell took them and disappeared for a moment. When he returned, he handed them to me with a smile. It was a nice smile allowing me to relax. The door buzzed, and Griggs held it open for me. There was a short hallway that opened to the shooting lanes.

It was smaller than the Reed Hill Gun Club, but it was nicer. There were five lanes with safety glass dividers. Griggs handed me the appropriate eye and ear protection. He then pointed me to one of the lanes.

"We have interactive targets, but we can start with the standard."

We spend an hour shooting. Griggs let me try all the different interactive targets. He even offered to set up a simulation that they used for police training. I declined that one. I enjoy shooting targets that obviously look like targets. I don't want to shoot anything that looks like a real person.

"You are good," Griggs said studying the results of my scores. All of the scoring was computerized. "Do you want a copy?"

"No. I just want to know if I beat you."

His mouth thinned and I knew I had. I tried to suppress a grin. Of course, he saw it and glared at me. I just laughed.

"I guess that means I owe you dinner," he said shortly.

CHAPTER 14

Still jubilant that I had shot better than he had, I agreed without thinking. We ended up at Antonio's. The same place Griggs had taken me the first and only other time we had dinner together. Antonio's is a locally owned casual Italian restaurant. You place your order at the counter, and someone brings it to the table. They do a lot of to-go orders as well as inside dining. As it was a Tuesday, the place wasn't very busy.

We didn't talk much at first. I was too hungry. The sandwich from lunch hadn't stayed with me long, and although it may not seem like it, shooting takes a lot of energy. Once I had satisfied my hunger, I sat back and studied Griggs. He has an attractive face, clean-shaven with sharp but pleasant features. His broad shoulders filled out his shirt nicely. The little butterflies, that seem to live in my stomach whenever he is around, started fluttering. He was considering the dessert menu and looked up when he felt my eyes on him.

"What?" he asked with a slight frown on his face.

"Nothing," I said hastily. A smile blossomed on his face as a knowing look entered his eyes. Those eyes darkened, and the butterflies started dancing even faster. I had to will the blush away. I needed to distract him. "Can you tell me anything about Donnie's case?"

Putting the menu down, he leaned back with a sigh. "Unfortunately, there's not much to tell. We don't have any real leads. Your buddy Sean was in the area at the time, but he has no motive. We couldn't find a connection between him and Donnie."

I clamped down on the guilt I was feeling. There might be a connection between Sean and Donnie. A connection I knew about but the police didn't. I had a bad feeling I was about to learn how far I was willing to go to keep my promise to Sean.

"Not even drugs?" I asked.

"No. Donnie doesn't appear to have been into drugs. We did find Sean's little hideaway at the north end of the woods. There were some cigarette butts and marijuana wrappers. I suspect that if it hadn't rained recently we'd have found something a little more serious." He paused and took a drink of his coffee. "Sean doesn't appear to be connected to the Cantonos."

I fiddled with the napkin I had laid on the table. "You think the Cantonos are still selling drugs?"

Griggs shrugged. "There's no evidence of that, but it's been their business for a while."

"Marcus said he was closing the family business."

"As much as you might want to believe it, I'm not sure Marcus is actually in charge of the family business."

Marcus had seemed in charge to me. Both of his nephews, Mike and Ricky, had appeared to be afraid of him. Or at least acknowledged him as someone to be obeyed.

"Ricky seemed to follow his lead. When they were at the store yesterday, Ricky told me he had told Donnie that Marcus had guaranteed my safety, that I was off-limits."

"Doesn't mean they aren't selling."

"Did you talk to Agent Martin?" James Martin is an agent with the FBI. He had recently been in Reed Hill to investigate the drug smuggling operation Raymond Hunter and Isabel Meeks had been running. Martin and Griggs had formed a good working relationship.

"I called him," Griggs said. "He hadn't heard any rumors

about the Cantonos, but they're small-time. Martin and the FBI would have never looked at Reed Hill if it hadn't been for Hunter."

When I didn't say anything, he continued. "As for Ricky, he has an alibi for the time in question, although it's a little shaky."

"What do you mean?"

"He spent the night with his girlfriend. She alibied him, but she isn't the most reliable witness."

"Why would Ricky be a suspect?" I asked.

"He and Donnie were friends." He used air quotes when he said the word friends. "And Ricky was the last person to have seen Donnie alive."

"Are Ricky and Sean your only two suspects?"

"We're looking into Donnie's life. He wasn't in town long enough to have many contacts. He probably had some enemies back in New York, but why would they come to Texas to murder him?"

"Maybe to not draw attention to themselves?"

"It's possible. We'll look at it. The NYPD is checking that angle, but it's a long shot. The only real clue we have is the ring."

"I just don't see why someone would kill Donnie for a fake ring."

"We don't know that they did. The ring might not have anything to do with the murder."

"But you think it does," I said slowly watching him. He nodded once. "Why?"

"The killer searched Donnie. Why hide the ring if it wasn't important? Nothing else makes sense. There's a lot of interest in that ring."

"Really?"

"Jose Alvera seemed fascinated by it, and when I showed it to a jeweler in Dallas, she asked me a ton of questions about where I got it."

"I told you my great-grandfather was fairly well-known for his designs, but I agree with you about Jose. His reaction was a little creepy."

"He did seem overly interested and not very helpful. The NYPD have also been checking with some jewelers in New York. Someone had to make the ring for Donnie unless he made it himself."

The only person I had spoken with about Donnie was Wade, and he hadn't indicated that Donnie had any talent along those lines. It doesn't mean he couldn't have made the ring, but the replica was precise. The stones and metal were obviously fake, but the design was accurate. It had to have been made by someone who had experience. When I said as much to Griggs, he agreed.

"The ring is the only thing we don't have an answer for," he said.

"That and his shoes," I muttered.

"What?"

"We don't know why the killer took his shoes."

Griggs grinned. "Actually, we do. Ross spoke with one of the detectives in the robbery division in New York. Apparently, Donnie liked old movies and television shows. He dressed in fancy suits and had shoes specially made with a hidden compartment in the heel."

"You have got to be kidding me!" I exclaimed.

"No," Griggs said with a laugh.

"That's ridiculous."

He nodded. "But it worked. They arrested Donnie several times near various crime scenes. A house would have been broken into and a small piece of jewelry, very fine jewelry mind you, would have been stolen. Only they never found it on Donnie. They searched his pockets and the lining of his clothes, even the inside of his shoes. But not the heels."

I shook my head. "How did they figure it out?"

"One day, they caught him red-handed, still in the house. He had managed to get his shoes back on but hadn't stuffed the heel well enough. When they picked up his shoe, it rattled."

Suddenly I started laughing. Griggs joined in. The release of tension felt good. I hadn't recognized how tense I had become over the past couple of days. The robbery and murder had affected me more than I realized.

"The killer had to have known Donnie, or at least, known about his shoes."

Griggs nodded. "He searched Donnie's pockets but didn't find anything so took the shoes thinking that the ring would be there."

"It sounds like something you would have seen on *Get Smart.*" I was still trying to control my laughter.

"I think Donnie was aiming for something a little more sophisticated," Griggs said with a grin. "More along the lines of Sam Spade than Maxwell Smart."

"That explains his clothes. I thought he dressed like a mobster."

"He did. In the old movies he liked, he identified with the gangster." Griggs glanced at the menu again. "It doesn't look like they have any strawberry pie, but would you like something else?"

We both ordered the tiramisu. We talked a little more until our desserts arrived. My mind kept going back to Donnie and his love of old movies. It reminded me of my love of mysteries. For some odd reason that made me smile. It was like we had some small thing in common. It also made me realize that I needed to make sure Donnie's killer was caught. The police found no connection between Donnie and Sean, but I was pretty sure I had. I fought with my conscience a few moments. It was time to come clean.

"Okay, I need to tell you something."

"That sounds ominous."

"Not really, but you're not going to be happy."

I took a deep breath and told Griggs what I had discovered. I told him about Sean and his new art and how one of the pieces looked almost exactly like one designed by Albert. The more I talked, the grimmer he looked. When I finished, he sat back in the booth and studied me. His deep green eyes pinned me in place.

"Why the hell didn't you tell us this sooner?" he snapped.

"I promised Sean I…" I couldn't go on. He was right. I should have told them. Even if it never amounted to anything, it was something the police needed to know. "I'm sorry."

"You sure know how to put a damper on an evening." He pulled out his phone and placed a call. While he spoke, I decided I had royally screwed up the whole day. Now both Aaron and Griggs were angry with me. The worst part was I couldn't blame either of them. My stomach roiled, and I lost my appetite. I pushed the half-eaten tiramisu away.

"Megan will talk to Sean," Griggs said as he disconnected the call. "Try to find out if there's a connection between the designs and Donnie."

"Alex," I said softly. He looked startled. I realized it was the first time I had called him by his first name. I swallowed. "I really am sorry I didn't say anything sooner."

"It's who you are," he said with a slight smile. "You're always trying to protect others. You're nosy but a good friend."

"I'm not nosy," I said indignantly. He started laughing again. It took me a moment, but I soon joined in.

"Can we talk about something else for a change?" Griggs asked, voice still full of amusement. "Something other than murder?"

"Like what?"

"Hell, I don't know. Anything else. Tell me about your birthday. How old are you anyway?"

"Yeah, like I'm going to tell you that!"

"I can just look it up," he said nonchalantly.

"Fine, look it up but I'm not telling you."

He smiled wickedly. "So what did you do on your thirty-fifth birthday?"

Exasperated, I opened my mouth and closed it again. My birthday had been something of a comedy of errors, and I wasn't sure I wanted to relive it. Griggs just watched me patiently as if he really wanted to hear the whole tale. So I told him about getting up and heading out to treat myself to a birthday breakfast only to find Pandora, shivering, wet, and half-starved. I told him about spending the rest of the morning at the vet's office to make sure she was okay. My afternoon shopping spree turned into a run to the pet store to get supplies. And my evening dinner with the Westons was spent getting Harry to trust me. Griggs laughed in all the right places, asked questions, and seemed genuinely interested.

"Well, it sounds like quite a day," he said when I finished. "I'm sorry I missed it. Are you ready to leave?"

The drive back to Scents and Sensibility was short and completed in a comfortable silence. I was still thinking about poor Donnie and his shoes when Griggs pulled up behind the store. It was close to nine so Kara and Myra were gone as were all the other merchants. My car was the only one still in the parking lot.

"Thanks for your help with Aaron and for dinner," I said as Griggs walked me to my car.

"My pleasure," he replied. "Do you want me to follow you home?"

"No, I'll be fine." I unlocked the car and opened the door before turning back. "Well, good night."

He stepped forward and boxed me in. I gripped the car door with one hand to steady myself. All the air left my body as he leaned toward me. His hand came up and slid through my hair before landing on the back of my neck. His lips brushed mine softly, slowly…once…twice. He pulled back, smiled, and gently kissed me once more.

"Don't leave town," he whispered before turning away.

"Alex." I managed to get out the name before he reached his car. He turned. "Are you going to follow up on that this time?"

"I would have followed up last time if you hadn't gone out with Cantono on New Year's Eve." With that terse statement, he got in his car and drove away.

CHAPTER 15

When I arrived home, Harry met me at the door in desperate need to go out. I grabbed his leash and glanced around the apartment. I didn't see any accidents and was relieved I had dodged a bullet. Harry came to me housebroken, but he's not used to spending hours locked up. I hadn't meant to leave him for so long. Although it was dark, I decided he deserved a long walk.

I avoid the park after dark. There are lights along the bike path and in the parking lot, but the walking trail itself is not well-lit. While there was little reported crime in the area, I wasn't willing to take any chances.

Harry and I headed through the apartment complex to the other side. I wasn't going to walk him in the park itself, but the block around the park has a lot of homes and businesses. There are streetlamps and lighting from the nearby houses. It wasn't that late, only a little after nine so I knew I wouldn't be the only one still out.

We walked past Sean's apartment. I looked for any signs of life, but the windows were all dark. I also didn't see his car. Either he hadn't arrived home yet or he had gone out again. I was tempted to knock on the door to see if anyone was home but wasn't sure what I would say to him if he was. The police had probably already tried to contact him. If Sean had spoken to the police, he wouldn't want to talk to me.

Harry and I started our walk around the park. It was interrupted several times while he did his business. The poor guy had a very full bladder. My apartment complex is on one end of the park. We turned to the left and then took a right and headed north on Parkwood before making the turn that would take us back home. The street on the other side of the park is Park Lane, and it is a residential section. The houses are very nice. Several of them are quite large and fairly expensive. And they all have oversized yards with a lot of space.

At the very end of the street on the corner nearest my apartment complex, there is one house that has an exceptionally large lot. Somehow the owners had been able to get a full lot and more than half of the one next to it. This caused the leftover lot to be much smaller than the others. Sitting on this smaller piece of land is a house that doesn't quite fit in with the ones around it. It's a small Cape Cod style home with a lovely flowerbed under the front window and a large cedar elm tree in the yard. The tree is as tall as the house, and gorgeous in the spring and fall.

When we reached the house, I was shocked, excited, and scared to see a for-sale sign on the lawn. Shocked because the houses along this street are seldom sold. Excited because I absolutely love the house. And scared because I was afraid I wouldn't be able afford it. I pulled my cell phone from my pocket and called my realtor. I had forgotten the hour but thankfully, she didn't seem to mind. She told me she would check on it first thing in the morning.

With a spring in my step, I turned to walk back home when I saw a solitary figure leave the apartment complex. Harry started to shake and pulled on the leash. I quieted him with a touch on the head.

"Shh, Harry. Let's see what he does." We watched as Sean crossed the street and entered the park. "Now what in the world is he up to?"

I looked around, but there was no one else in the area.

Pulling Harry along, I, too, crossed the street and followed Sean down the path. The lighting along the walking trail is sparse. I usually carry a small flashlight with me if I go out after dark, but in my haste to get Harry outside, I had forgotten it. Carefully, I made my way down the path.

There was an eerie silence the deeper into the park I went. I could hear the whisper of the trees and the occasional snap of a twig under my foot. What was unnerving was the absolute absence of any other noise. No birdsong, no rustle of a shrub, no footfalls but my own. My heart began beating uncomfortably fast. There was nothing threatening me, but the flight instinct was in full force. I willed myself forward all the while wondering what I was doing. Harry trotted alongside me without a care in the world. It was then I realized I was trembling. I stopped on the path and was about to turn around when it hit me. I laughed silently. All the books I had read and all the movies I had seen came to me in a flash. I had worked myself up for nothing.

"Well, Harry," I said softly. "I just about managed to scare myself to death."

Harry wagged his tail and grinned. I got my breathing under control and moved forward. I could not see Sean anywhere along the path. I reached one of the benches and settled down to wait. There was no lamp nearby so I was sitting in darkness broken only by the light of the moon. It was…peaceful. If Sean was still in the park, he would return this way on his way home.

I extended Harry's leash and allowed him to move around. He wandered off into the bushes to investigate while I pulled out my phone and checked my email. I was reviewing Scents and Sensibility's online orders when a noise reached my ears. I glanced up, expecting Sean, and caught my breath when Ricky Cantono came into view. He didn't see me at first, and I was hoping he would continue to walk on by, but the light of my phone caught his eye. He was carrying a flashlight and raised it so that it shone in my face. I raised my arm, covering my eyes, temporarily blinded.

"Hey," I exclaimed. The light fell, but it took me a moment to stop seeing spots. When I could finally see again, Ricky was not three feet from me. The look on his face made my mouth go dry. All the earlier fear and tension came rushing back. I started to stand up but my legs felt unsteady. I forced strength into them and rose.

In a flash, Harry came charging out of the bushes, barked once, and stopped in front of me. Ricky jumped back just a little. If I hadn't been trying to control my trembling, it would have been funny. It didn't take Ricky long to recover. He glared at me before saying, "What the hell you doing here, bitch?"

Bitch. His brother, Mike, had called me the same thing back in December. I didn't like the slur, but did they really think that was such a terrible insult? I hear far worse on television. Couldn't they be more creative? If I was trying to intimidate someone, calling them a bitch wouldn't have been my first choice.

"You and Mike need to work on your vocabulary," I said shortly. I felt light-headed but was pleased to hear my voice sounded normal.

"What?" Ricky scowled at me not sure where to go with my statement. I'm pretty sure he was expecting me to fall to my knees begging him not to hurt me or to run away screaming. I did consider both briefly but held my ground.

"What are *you* doing here?" I asked. I could almost see the wheels turning in his head. He was trying to think of an excuse. I waited patiently. Nothing. Instead, he turned and started to walk away. "Where's Sean?"

My voice sounded raw as I was beginning to get worried. Ricky turned back and then took two steps toward me. When Harry growled softly, he stopped.

"You need to mind your own business, bitch. Marcus can't protect you from everything."

I stood on shaking knees as he walked away. I wiped my sweaty hand on my jeans and got a tighter hold on Harry's leash. I needed to find Sean.

Harry and I started walking in the direction Ricky had come from when a flash of light shone through the trees. I heard rustling and then a couple of choice swear words. My entire body relaxed as Sean stepped out and onto the path. He stopped suddenly when he saw me waiting.

"Leah?" he said.

"Sean."

"What are you doing here?"

"I could ask you the same thing."

He moved awkwardly and took a couple of steps forward. He was now on the path and walked over to where Harry and I stood. Harry nudged his hand and Sean absently petted him. I could tell he was stalling for time, trying to think of something to tell me.

"I just wanted to, you know, stretch my legs a little before going to bed. I have been driving all day. I went to visit some friends in San Antonio and just got back."

I studied him a moment. There was something off. Of course, I was expecting him to be hiding something. He shifted uncomfortably under my scrutiny.

"Sean," I said softly. "What's going on?"

"Nothing, Leah," he said rapidly. "Nothing at all."

"Okay. I stopped by your apartment to see you on Sunday. I wanted to look at your new sculptures again."

That caused him to pause. He was thinking so loud I could almost hear him. "Why?"

"They reminded me of one that I have. Or had. It was a wooden, hand-carved rose."

It was hard to tell in the dark, but he appeared to pale. His eyes widened, and he froze for a painful second. His mouth opened and closed again. I waited, hoping he would give some clue as to how he was involved, but he forced a smile and stepped away.

"Sean, the police know about the designs. They want to talk to you."

He stopped suddenly, looked at me with a wild-eyed expression, and then slumped his shoulders in defeat. He walked over to the bench and sat down, burying his face in his hands. I sat down beside him. When he still didn't say anything, I placed my hand on his arm.

"Where did you get the designs, Sean?"

"Ricky," he replied in a whisper.

I thought about that a minute. Ricky must have gotten the designs from Donnie and passed them along to Sean. But why? What did Albert's designs have to do with anything?

"Sean, please tell me what's going on. I'll try to help you if I can."

He lifted his head and looked at me. I tried to give him a reassuring smile. Sean and his designs were the first real clue I had found.

"About a month ago," Sean said slowly, "Ricky contacted me. We went to high school together, and I have been buying f…"

"You've been buying drugs from him," I said nonchalantly. I didn't want him to clam up.

He nodded. "I used to, but when most of his family was arrested back in December, I had to find someone else."

"Who did you find?" I don't know why I asked that question. I really didn't care where Sean was getting his supply. When he looked at me, I raised a hand. "Sorry, never mind."

"Anyway, Ricky asked to meet. He told me he would get me what I needed if I would carve a wooden rose for a friend. I told him I didn't work in wood, but he was…very persuasive."

"Did he tell you why he wanted it?"

"No," Sean said. "Just that a friend of his needed it. He sent me several designs so that I could practice creating something out of wood. My first couple of efforts weren't very good, but I got better. I started to enjoy it. The designs he sent me were really well done. The lion was the first piece I thought was good. So I then created the rose. I did the others that you saw later."

"What happened to the rose?" I asked.

He looked away at that. I saw his hands clench. He shook

them out and rubbed along his legs. Sean took a deep breath and spoke in a voice so soft I had to strain to hear him. "I gave it to Donnie."

Stunned, I sat back. I didn't doubt what he was saying, but I was surprised. Why would Donnie want a fake copy of both the ring and the rose? How were they connected?

"When, Sean? When did you give the rose to Donnie?"

"The day he was killed," he whispered.

"You saw him that morning?" He nodded. "Why didn't you tell the police?"

He looked at me incredulously. "They already suspected me. If I had told them I met with Donnie, they would've arrested me."

"Sean, did you kill Donnie?" My heart rate rose and my mouth went dry. Was I sitting in a dark park with a murderer?

"No!" he said with absolute surety. "Leah, I give you my word. I did not kill him."

I just stared at him. Was he telling me the truth? I thought so. He was young and naïve, but I didn't think he was a killer. Of course, Candace had surprised me as well.

"See," he said sadly when I didn't respond. "If you won't believe me, why would the police?"

"I do believe you, Sean, but you have to know you look guilty. You need to talk to the police and tell them everything." He nodded again, a little slower this time. "Sean, do you have any idea why Donnie wanted the rose made?"

"No. He never said. I barely spoke with him. Just that one time. I gave him the rose, he put it in his backpack, and I left."

"Wait, what? He had a backpack?"

"Yeah."

There had not been a backpack when I found Donnie, and Griggs never mentioned finding one. The killer must have taken it along with the shoes.

"Leah, what should I do?" Sean asked. He sounded so young.

I picked up my phone and called Griggs. I spent the next twenty minutes waiting with Sean until the police arrived.

Megan seemed a little put out that I had contacted Griggs. I had forgotten she was in charge of the case. Griggs, himself, tried to stay out of the way. He spoke with me briefly but didn't say much otherwise. Megan asked me and Sean a couple of cursory questions and then took Sean away. I didn't know what they could possibly charge him with, but I had a feeling Sean was going to spend the night in jail.

CHAPTER 16

The rain was back the next day. It wasn't the downpour we had the week before but a steady rain that made the streets slick and driving unpleasant. I never saw any lightning, but a couple of loud claps of thunder had woken my companions and me. Pandora is not afraid of a fifty-pound dog, but thunder and heavy winds frighten her. Harry sleeps in his own bed in a corner of my room, but Pandora sleeps on the pillow beside me. At the first rumble, she jumped straight up in the air and landed on my head before streaking across the bed and then diving under it.

This, of course, woke Harry who decided he needed to go out. I was still feeling guilty for leaving him alone for so long the day before so I threw on some clothes and headed downstairs. Harry and I huddled under an umbrella in the grassy area near my apartment while he did his business. Neither of us was happy about it.

It was too early to go into work so I made breakfast and sat down at the table with my notebook. It had been a while since I had updated my notes and a lot had happened. After reading through what I had, I found that I was having trouble keeping the timeline straight. According to Sean, Ricky had contacted him about a month ago to start working on the rose sculpture, but Donnie hadn't arrived in town until late Tuesday and was killed on Thursday morning after getting the rose from Sean. What took him so long to contact Sean? Wednesday seemed completely unaccounted for. I made a note to ask Ricky what Donnie had been doing that day.

Leon broke into my apartment on Sunday. It appeared now that he was after the rose. It's possible that the two weren't connected, but I had a hard time convincing myself of that. So if the killer took the rose Sean made from Donnie, why did he need mine? And what was the connection between the rose and my great-grandmother's ruby ring? Other than they both belonged to the same person and were made by the two brothers, I couldn't see any link.

I wondered if the police had learned who had made the fake ring for Donnie. If so, perhaps that person would know why Donnie needed it. Griggs said the NYPD was talking to jewelers about the ring. I made another note to ask Griggs.

I glanced at the clock. I still had an hour before I needed to be at work. That gave me just enough time to call Marcus. I needed to know what Ricky knew about the rose. He hadn't said anything to me about the ring, but then I hadn't asked. I hadn't known at the time if Ricky or Marcus knew anything about the ring, and Griggs had wanted to keep it out of the public's knowledge. But Ricky had to know about the rose since he gave the design sketches to Sean. I also wanted to know if Marcus knew anything he hadn't told me.

"Hello, Leah," he said sounding resigned.

"Sorry to call you so early."

"It's not early. What can I do for you?"

I paused. How much had Ricky told him? I decided to plunge right in. "Did Ricky tell you about last night?"

There was a moment of silence. "What about last night?"

"I saw him in the park with Sean Walters."

"Why do I know that name?"

I explained who he was and that I had asked Ricky about him when Marcus had brought Ricky by the store. Instead of waiting for his questions, I told Marcus everything. I knew that

Marcus wanted to protect his nephew, but in order to do so, he needed all the information. He released a few swear words as I was speaking. The more I talked, the less he said until he was completely silent.

"Did you know any of this?" I asked as I finished.

"No," Marcus growled. He sounded angry. "I can't believe he's selling again."

"I don't know that he is, Marcus. I'm just telling you what Sean said. He said Ricky would get him what he needed if he created the wooden rose for Donnie."

"What else could it mean, Leah?" I had no answer to that. I did believe that Ricky was paying Sean with drugs of some kind. Marcus took my silence for agreement and continued, "Why is this rose so important?"

"I don't know, Marcus. If I did, it might explain a few things."

"I'll talk to Ricky. No promises, but I'll see if I can find out what's going on. He's been avoiding me. I had to hunt him down to bring him by your store the other day."

"You sound tired," I said. It bothered me that Marcus was hurting. My pseudo date with Griggs hadn't resolved my feelings about Marcus. There was still something there between us. I just wished I knew what it was.

I heard him sigh. "I'm having issues with the restaurant. Working crazy hours. I don't need Ricky to screw up."

"I'm sorry," I said softly.

"Not your fault. Thanks for letting me know."

"Marcus," I called before he could hang up. "Let me know what you find out."

"I will, Leah."

Checking my notes one last time, I decided there was nothing more I could do. I got dressed, bundled Harry into the car, and headed for work. The back door buzzer rang not long after I arrived. I opened the door to find Finley waiting. Finley is a delivery driver for the company we use to ship our products. He has been the driver on the route for my store for over five years and knew exactly what to do. I moved aside and propped the door open as he unloaded boxes. It didn't take him long as the delivery was small. This wasn't a busy time for us so we didn't need to restock as much. When he was done, I asked if he had time for coffee.

"I heard a rumor about a body in the park," he said when I handed him his coffee.

"You heard about that?" I asked with a grimace.

Finley doesn't live in town, but as a delivery driver, he knows a lot of people. Reed Hill is still small enough that news gets around fast. Especially in the downtown area where we all see each other every day. It wasn't at all surprising that Finley knew I had found Donnie in the park.

"Of course I heard," he said echoing my thought. "I had a delivery at Reed Hill Crafts on Friday. Stella told me all about it."

Stella is the manager at Reed Hill Crafts which is located on the other side of the square. I didn't go over there often but had met Stella at some of the merchant meetings. I like her. She and Finley seemed to be having a lot of conversations lately. He had been bringing up her name a lot.

Finley is a good-looking guy. He has skin the color of milk chocolate, a beautiful smile, and a wicked sense of humor. He had told me he was tired of the bar scene and wanted to know where he could meet a nice girl. I couldn't help him as my dating life wasn't exactly stellar. He seemed to have resolved the issue by himself.

"Tell me what happened," he said gently. Although there is no romantic attraction between the two of us, we are good friends. He wasn't being nosy—just giving me an opportunity to talk.

I settled in my chair and told him everything. It was nice to talk it all out. I had discussed bits and pieces with both Olivia and Griggs, but telling Finley everything from the beginning helped me organized my thoughts.

"That Jose is a weird dude," Finley said when I had finished. "I saw him Monday evening arguing with some guy."

"Really? Who?"

"Not sure," Finley replied. "It was after work. I had stopped by Antonio's to get a bite to eat before going home. Monday is lasagna night."

Antonio's offers a discount on two of their specialties during the week. Mondays it was lasagna. Wednesdays it was fettuccine. I grinned at Finley. He loved the lasagna, and I loved the fettuccine.

"Anyway, I had to park near the back," he continued. "Jose and the other guy were in the parking lot behind Carson's Auto Repair."

"They were arguing?"

"Yeah. It was dark so I couldn't see real well. I think the argument got pretty heated. I couldn't hear what they were saying, but their voices were raised and there was a lot of gesturing. The other guy was a lot bigger than Jose. 'Course, Jose's a small man. I thought about intervening, but Jose said something to him and they both walked away."

"I wonder what that was all about."

"No idea, but it was weird."

"Can you give me a general description of the guy with Jose?"

"Well, like I said he was big. White guy. I didn't get a good look at his face, but he had a bandage on his hand."

I sat up. A bandage? Monday night after work, Finley had said. It could have easily been Leon. Griggs said they didn't arrest him until late that evening. I described Myra's ex-husband, and Finley nodded.

"Yeah, it could've been him," he said as he stood. "I better get going. I have a light schedule today, but the rain makes it slow going. Thanks for the coffee."

"Be careful."

So now we had a connection between Leon and Jose, who knew about my ring. I called Griggs to tell him what Finley had said. He didn't answer so I left a short message. We knew Leon stole my rose, and that Donnie had a fake version of the ring and the rose created. If Leon killed Donnie but couldn't find the fake ring on him, maybe Leon hired Jose to create a copy of the ring. If so, why? It kept coming back to what was so special about great-grandmother Rose's ring.

With the rain, we didn't have very many customers so it was a slow day for us. I process payroll on Wednesday. Normally I come in late and stay after we close, but as Emma was on vacation, I was working a split shift. After Kara came back from lunch, I left for a few hours. Harry was content to spend the afternoon in the back room of the store. I was planning to spend my afternoon in the library, but before that I wanted to speak with Jose.

Like Scents and Sensibility, Gemstones wasn't very busy. There was only one customer there when I walked in. I asked for Jenny, but her assistant told me she was at lunch. However, Jose was working.

Since Jenny and I had become friends, I was in Gemstones occasionally. I knew the store layout pretty well. I wasn't really trying to sneak up on Jose, but I did want to see what he was working on. I stood in the doorway of the back room. Jose was sitting at the bench, hunched over something with pliers in his hand. I couldn't see the piece he was working on, but it was set in some type of device that held it in place.

I must have made a noise because Jose suddenly jumped, twisted his head around, and saw me standing there. I gave him a weak smile. He quickly turned away, grabbed a cloth, and covered the piece. He then turned to face me.

"Sorry I startled you," I said as I stepped into the room. He didn't reply. "What are you working on?"

"Nothing," he said and then blushed. "I mean, it's a piece for a private customer."

"Oh, I see." I glanced around casually. There were several pieces of paper on the bench, but all were overlapping. I tried to see the designs, but Jose leaned over, blocking them.

"So," I continued, "a friend of mine said he saw you last Monday night behind Carson's Auto Repair talking to Leon Hollins. I didn't know you knew Leon."

Jose's eyes widened in horror. His face paled and his eyes darted around the room. He swallowed and croaked out, "I don't. I mean, it wasn't me."

"You weren't talking to Leon?"

"Don't know any Leon."

"Oh, my friend seemed pretty sure it was you." I laughed lightly. "Maybe it was your double. Do you know anyone who looks like you?"

"No, no one. Who saw me?" He seemed to have recovered his composure. He was glaring at me now and getting a little worked up. He stood and took a step toward me in a threatening manner. Jose's not a large man, but he was certainly stronger than me. "Who was it?"

"I just heard it in passing," I said, moving back toward the door. There was no way I was going to throw Finley under the bus. Jose was acting weird, even for him. I wasn't exactly afraid, but I was concerned. Thinking quickly, I tried to find an excuse for questioning him. "Look, Jose, I'm sorry if I upset you. Leon is Myra's ex-husband, and he threatened her. I'm worried he may try to hurt her so I was hoping you might be able to help. If he threatened you too…"

Jose stared at me a moment, and then shook his head. His body relaxed, and he returned to the chair. He turned his back to me saying dismissively, "Wasn't me."

Thankful he seemed to let it go, I quickly made my getaway. I had no doubt in my mind Jose had lied to me, but I wasn't about to confront him again. I left the store and ran to my car. Spending the afternoon in the peaceful confines of the library was looking even more attractive.

CHAPTER 17

Reed Hill Public Library is just a few blocks away from the square. If the weather is nice, I sometimes walk to it on my lunch break, but as it was still raining, I drove my car. I love to read and although I read a lot of books electronically, I still enjoyed spending time at the library.

I spoke briefly with one of the librarians and then found a quiet corner to while away the afternoon. I had been there about an hour when some rapid, angry whispering caught my attention. I couldn't make out the words, but the voices were familiar.

Looking around, I didn't see anyone. I turned my head trying to pinpoint the location. It took me a moment, but I finally determined they were near the back wall. Although I was curious to know who was there, I tried not to eavesdrop. I returned to my book with one eye on the doorway. The room I was in was fairly large, but there was only one way to enter or leave. I had a perfect view from my seat.

The whispering continued for a few more minutes before ending in a terse punctuation. A moment later, a man stepped out from behind the last aisle. His back was to me so I couldn't see his face. He was a large man wearing a raincoat with the collar up and a hat pulled down low on his head. There was something familiar about him. The rain outside was reason enough for the coat and hat, but it appeared to me he was trying to not be recognized. I got up, gathered my things, and started to follow. After taking a couple of steps, I paused. There was no reason for me to follow the man, I told myself. I could justify being curious about a whispered conversation because it caught my attention, but following some guy I didn't know was pushing it.

A movement by the entrance caught my attention. Ricky Cantono walked out from behind the aisle. What was he doing in the library? Ricky did not strike me as the literary type. A clandestine meeting in the library didn't seem his style. He would more likely meet someone in a dark alley. Something was going on and Ricky knew more about Donnie than he was telling me. This time I didn't hesitate to follow.

The library doors closed behind me just in time for me to see Ricky crossing the street headed toward the downtown square. I glanced at the skies. The rain was lighter, but a steady drizzle was still coming down. My umbrella was large and bright so it would be easy to spot. I hurried to my car, dumped my things, and pulled out a black, light-weight rain jacket. Slipping it on, I pulled up the hood and walked down the street.

At first, I thought I had lost him, but when I got to the corner of Main and Pine, I glanced south and saw him entering the secondary parking garage. The main parking garage for the downtown area is across the street from my store. Most of the store employees and many of our customers park there, but there is a second, smaller garage on Pine. I didn't want Ricky to see me so I circled around back and looked through the opening. He was talking on his phone and facing Pine so I slipped in and hurried halfway down the aisle.

Ricky abruptly ended his conversation so I ducked between two cars and crouched down. It was at that exact moment I realized I had screwed up. If Ricky or anyone else walked past, they would see me. If I stood, Ricky would see me. I was trapped.

I was close enough I could hear him moving. I tried to picture myself standing and nonchalantly walking out of the garage. I didn't think I could pull it off. I would have to wait him out. With a sigh, I got on my hands and knees and crawled toward the front of the cars. I was lucky. The driver of the car on my right had not pulled all the way in. I wedged myself between the bumper of the car and the wall and settled down to wait. Hopefully the owner of the car wouldn't be back anytime soon.

One of the things I don't like about some of the mysteries I read is how the heroine gets herself into ridiculous situations. I leaned my head back on the wall and laughed silently. Here I was in my own ridiculous situation because I couldn't keep my nose out of someone else's business. The only thing worse would be if Griggs showed up and caught me. I could just imagine that conversation.

"'Bout time." I heard Ricky say. Someone else answered, but they were too far away for me to hear what they said. Ricky must have moved closer to the entrance.

"He…ring…now," Ricky said. He sounded agitated and nervous. The other person answered in a low voice.

Ring? Were they talking about Rose's ring or giving someone a ring—like a phone call? I leaned to the right, trying to hear.

"…working….delicate…more time."

"How…we don't ha…time."

The other man, and I thought it was a male because of the voice, mumbled something else. They continued along that vein for a few minutes. I could only hear about every fourth or fifth word. I did hear the word ring repeated twice as well as needing more time. The conversation got louder when Ricky lost his patience. I heard him quite clearly. "Twenty-four hours! Get it to us or he'll find you. You don't want him to find you."

His voice sent a slight chill down my spine. He wasn't as good at intimidation as Marcus, but he was still pretty good. He must have walked away because I then heard only one voice muttering. There was some cursing and at least one derogatory name that I could make out. The most interesting part was it was all in Spanish. Who did I know who spoke Spanish and was interested in my great-grandmother's ring?

A few minutes later, all was silent. I eased my way out and slowly stood, peeking over the car hood before standing fully. I was alone. I quickly made my way to my car and drove back to Scents and Sensibility.

It was almost four, and the store was busier than it had been earlier. Myra was scheduled to leave at four, but she agreed to stay while I made one more stop. I hurried over to Gemstones to speak with Jenny.

I entered the back room and saw Jose sitting at his workbench. I couldn't tell if his hair was wet, but there was a jacket hanging on his chair that looked damp and small drops of water on the floor. He was still hunched over the piece I had seen him working on earlier. He looked up when I walked in and his eyes narrowed. I greeted him briefly but only received a grunt in return. He turned back to the item in front of him without a word to me. Giving him a wide berth, I hurried over to knock on Jenny's open office door. She gave me a slight smile.

"Hi, Leah."

"Hey, Jenny," I replied. "Got a minute?"

"Sure."

I stepped into her office and closed the door behind me. Her eyes widened just a fraction, but she didn't comment as I made my way over to the chair and sat.

"Has Jose been here all afternoon?"

Jenny frowned. She sat back in her chair and looked at me a moment. "He got a phone call and then took a brief break. He got back about ten minutes ago."

Was Jose really involved with Donnie's murder? I thought about it a moment. He was an odd little man and had seemed exceptionally interested in my ring, but there was nothing to indicate he was violent. However, he had some type of relationship with Leon. That didn't look good. Griggs had said the killer had to have been a fairly large person to break

Donnie's neck. Jose was about my height so I knew he wasn't the killer. That didn't mean he wasn't involved—if the ring and the murder were connected. I was now pretty sure they were, and Griggs seemed convinced.

"Leah," Jenny said, interrupting my thoughts. "What's going on?"

Jenny listened as I told her what I had heard. She was even kind enough not to laugh when I mentioned hiding between cars in the garage. I thought I saw her mouth twitch, but Jenny is hard to read. When I had first met her, I thought she was always serious and didn't have much of a sense of humor. Having gotten to know her better, I realized she had a great sense of humor. It was just dry and very low-key. Her eyes danced in amusement, but she didn't laugh out loud.

"Jose's a little weird," she said when I had finished. "I don't think he has done anything wrong, but I did see him talking to a guy I think is Myra's ex-husband."

"You did? When?"

"On Monday." The same day he had threatened Myra, and the same day that Finley had seen Leon talking to Jose.

"And it was Leon?" I asked her.

"I think so. He looked like the guy the police arrested."

"Did he have a bandage on his right hand?" At her nod, I continued, "That's Leon. He's the one who broke into my apartment. If Jose was talking to him, then maybe Leon was after the ring. And Jose is involved."

"I don't know, Leah," Jenny said. "Jose's worked here for two years, and we've never had a problem. I did a background check on him before I hired him, and we do annual rechecks."

"So maybe he was talking to Leon about something else? Maybe Ricky was threatening him about another ring? He seemed pretty upset. Could Ricky have ordered a ring or requested an appraisal?" I was afraid Ricky had commissioned Jose to make another ring designed exactly like Rose's. If Ricky had, he had something to do with both the ring and the wooden rose.

"Not through Gemstones," Jenny replied to my question.

"I've never had any of the Cantonos in the store. Are you sure it was Jose talking to Ricky?"

"Pretty sure. It's too much of a coincidence that he returned from break only a few minutes after I thought I heard him with Ricky."

"Coincidences do happen," Jenny said. There was a short pause. "Look, Leah, I trust you. You helped me and Trent when we needed it. But I remember what it was like to be a suspect when I hadn't done anything wrong. I don't want Jose or anyone else to have to go through that."

Jenny had been questioned several times concerning Isabel's death, mostly in connection to Trent's alibi. She even had to hire a lawyer. It was an unpleasant time. I could understand her concern, but I was convinced that Jose had been speaking to Ricky.

"I understand," I said. "Has Jose done anything unusual lately? Anything that you might be concerned about?"

She was silent a moment. Her face was completely empty of expression, but she didn't look at me. She reached out and picked up a pen that was lying on the desk in front of her. Twisting it in her hand, she finally looked me in the eye.

"He's been working a lot of extra hours," she said slowly. "Jose doesn't design new pieces, but he does repairs and will reset or replace stones for customers. He's only scheduled for forty hours a week, but sometimes, when he has a special order, he will work extra hours. We don't have any special orders this week. Yet, he stayed late Monday and Tuesday and came in early yesterday and today."

"Do you know what he's working on?"

Jenny shook her head. "When I asked him, he said he was working on something for a friend. He does that sometimes. Some of the equipment he uses belongs to the store, but some of it is his own. If he wants to work on a piece of jewelry, he usually does it here."

"So if Ricky hired him to make a copy of my great-grandmother's ring…"

"He might work on it here," Jenny finished for me. When

she looked at me this time, her eyes were sad. "Leah, he has a large family he's helping to support. Even if he is working on something for Ricky, it doesn't mean it's your great-grandmother's ring, and it doesn't mean he's doing anything illegal."

I thought Jenny was being naïve, but I wasn't going to change her mind. She had the same attitude when everyone thought Trent had killed Isabel. She refused to believe that he could have done anything wrong.

"You're right," I said to appease her. "Maybe I could talk to him. Feel him out so to speak. I don't want to say anything to the police if it wasn't him."

"How are you going to find out?" Jenny asked. "You can't just come out and ask him. He'll think you're crazy."

"I'll be subtle," I said standing.

Finally, Jenny laughed and stood also. "This I have to see."

"Hey! I can be subtle," I said reaching for the door. I opened it and stepped out only to find Jose nowhere in sight. I turned to look at Jenny. She shook her head.

"He usually works until closing," she said.

His jacket was gone. I walked over to the bench. Everything appeared to be in order. I asked Jenny to check, and she said nothing appeared out of place to her. Before I went back to Scents and Sensibility, I checked the main parking garage. Jose's car was missing. It looked like he flew the coop.

CHAPTER 18

By the time I got back to the store, it was four thirty. I sent Myra home and helped Kara with customers. It wasn't until after we had closed and Kara had gone home that I had time to consider what I had learned. I needed to inform the police. I reached for my phone to call Griggs and paused. Megan was in charge of the investigation. She hadn't seemed very happy when I called Griggs about Sean. She had given me her card and made a point of telling me to contact her if I had any new information. This was her first case. I decided it would be best if I called her.

"Ms. Norwood," she said after I identified myself.

"Captain Ross," I said with a slight smile. Although I didn't know her well, she would always be Megan to me.

"How can I help you?" she asked.

I launched into my story and told her about my afternoon. There was a long pause on the line. "Okay, let me see if I have this straight. You followed Ricky Cantono to a parking garage where he met with a man you think was Jose Alvera about a ring you think might be like one our victim had. You then planned to question Mr. Alvera only to find him gone."

"Yes," I said softly. She didn't sound pleased. Maybe I should have called Griggs after all.

"Where are you now?"

"At the store."

"Can you come by the station for an interview?"

"Uh, sure, but I need to process payroll for my employees first. Once I'm done, I can come by."

She huffed out a breath. "I'll come to you. Sit tight."

I completed the payroll and took Harry for a short walk around the parking lot. Across from the parking lot is a condominium building. Dividing the parking lot and the condo is a small strip of grass with a few trees scattered in. Harry used the area when we didn't have time for a longer walk. We were headed back into the store when a dark sedan pulled up. Megan opened the driver's door, and Griggs got out of the passenger side. I wasn't surprised to see him. He had said he would be shadowing Megan.

Without saying a word, I opened the door to the store, and they followed me inside. Harry greeted Griggs and tried to get Megan's attention. Once again she was studiously avoiding him. I didn't remember her being so dog-averse in the park. Maybe it was the close quarters. I got Harry settled on his bed and then sat down myself.

Griggs stood by the door while Megan took the chair opposite me and said, "Tell me again what happened this afternoon."

I retold my story, trying not to blush when I got to the part about hiding between the cars. Griggs snorted softly. Megan's face was carefully blank although I'm sure she found it amusing as well. She interrupted a couple of times to clarify a point, but it didn't take long for me to finish. No one said anything for a few minutes as Megan completed her notes.

"Okay. I think I have everything. You're sure you didn't see the man Cantono met?"

"Yes, I'm sure."

"Jose Alvera isn't at home," Griggs added. "He lives alone so he could just be out somewhere. We can't issue an APB as he hasn't been reported missing, and you can't verify that it was him. There's no proof he has done anything. We don't want to contact his family yet. No need to worry them."

"But you think it was him?"

Griggs opened his mouth to speak but quickly closed it again. He looked at Megan and waited. She seemed surprised he had stopped. I hid a smile. Griggs was trying not to take over the case, but it had to be hard.

"We don't know," Megan replied. "What else can you tell us about the man in the library?"

"Nothing, really."

"You said he seemed familiar."

"Yes, but like I said, I didn't get a look at his face."

Griggs stepped forward. "What about him seemed familiar?"

"I don't know. The way he moved, I guess. His build. I wish I could tell you more, but it was more of a feeling."

"You said he was wearing a coat and a hat. Can you describe them?"

"The coat was one of those gray vinyl ones. Thin but full length."

"So it was probably cheap," Megan said and looked at Griggs. "Maybe a throwaway."

Griggs nodded and looked back at me. "What about the hat? Was it a baseball cap, a cowboy hat?"

I shook my head. "No. It had a wide brim. I think it was cotton, like one of those you see tour guides wearing. Easy to care for but sturdy."

"Okay. I don't think his clothes will help us any, but we can put out a general description for the patrol units. Can you give us anything else? Hair color, skin color, height, weight?"

"Pssh." I blew out a breath. That was harder. "Well, he was white. I couldn't see his hair so it was shorter than the hat. He was tall and big. Over six feet. Not fat, just big."

Megan nodded. I waited but that was all I got. Griggs might be willing to talk to me about the case, but Megan wasn't saying anything.

"That's all I can remember. I'll call you if I think of anything else."

"Thank you," she replied. "Just a word of advice, Ms. Norwood. It might be smart not to follow anyone else."

I rolled my eyes but nodded. Megan rose and headed to the door. I stood as well. Griggs told her he would be out in a minute. She gave me a polite smile and left.

"Leon Hollins made bail this afternoon."

Of all the things I thought he might say, that was not one of them. I stared at him, dumbfounded. "What?"

"Hollins is out of jail. He made bail."

"Does Myra know?"

"David went to talk to her. He wants her to file a restraining order. We let Hollins know that we'd be watching him, but it might be prudent to have Myra stay with you again."

"I'll call her before I leave."

"You need to be careful, too. It was your apartment he robbed."

I shuddered. I was a fairly independent person, but I tried not to be reckless. Leon might not be after me personally, but he was a dangerous man. And scary.

"You're convinced the theft is related to the murder. Do you think he killed Donnie?"

"It's possible. He's large enough, and he was in the military."

"What does that have to do with it?"

"The way Donnie's neck was broken is a technique they teach in the Marines."

"How do you know that?"

His eyes went distant. For the first time since I met him, I realized that Griggs had scars that I couldn't see. He didn't answer my question but looked down at Harry sleeping on the dog bed. When he looked back at me, his eyes were clear. "You said Harry reacted badly to him. The wound on Hollins's hand was a dog bite. Keep Harry close."

I nodded. "I will. If Myra and I stick together, I doubt he'll do anything."

"Hopefully not." He opened the door and paused. "Are

you free Friday night?"

"Um, yes?"

His eyes traveled down my body and back up again. He gave me a slow, sensuous smile. "Are you sure?"

I narrowed my eyes and frowned. "Yes, I'm sure. Why?"

"I'll pick you up at seven," he said and walked out, closing the door behind him.

"For what?" I muttered, but I couldn't keep the smile off my face. I sat back down and basked in the moment. He was finally following through.

My thoughts soon turned back to Leon. I grabbed my phone and called Myra. We talked for a few minutes. She was hesitant to leave her animals again. The cats could probably fend for themselves, but the horses needed daily attention. I didn't want her to be alone so I offered to stay with her if Pandora and Harry could come as well. Myra immediately agreed. She didn't want to be alone any more than I did.

Harry and I went by my apartment to pack a few things and pick up Pandora. She wasn't too thrilled to be bundled into the cat carrier again, but I refused to leave her alone. Myra and I spent the rest of the evening rehashing the case and talking about what we would do if Leon did show up. I didn't think he would. He was a bully, but Myra had called his bluff. In my experience, that's usually enough.

The next day passed quickly. Myra and I drove into work together as I was staying at her house. Thursday is Kara's day off so we both grabbed a sandwich from Nora's for lunch. The store wasn't too busy so we had time to take a break. We spent most of the day restocking the shelves and organizing the back room.

A call to Marcus went unanswered. I left him a message telling him that Ricky had met with someone concerning a ring and could he ask him about it. There was no sign of Jose at Gemstones. Of course, he wasn't scheduled to work again until Friday, but I did wheedle his home address out of Jenny.

By the time we were ready to close the store, I had not heard back from Marcus. I wasn't sure what to think about that. I hoped he wasn't ignoring me, but he had made it clear that family came first for him. Every time we spoke, I was basically accusing his nephew of something. I was afraid our short-lived friendship was already over.

"Would you mind if we drove by Jose's house?" I asked Myra as we were leaving.

She glanced at me from the passenger's seat. "You want to visit Jose?"

"I want to see if he's come home. Griggs said he wasn't home yesterday."

"Okay, where does he live?"

"Over on River Street."

I made a left out of the parking lot and headed south on Elm. Jose lived in a section of town near Gabe's manufacturing plant. It was a large neighborhood with a lot of starter homes. Just as I was about to turn onto River Street, a motorcycle flew past us, going way too fast for a residential street. It was after six so it was already dark, but I caught a glimpse of the rider's profile. I gasped softly.

"What?" Myra asked.

"That was Ricky Cantono."

"What's he doing in this neighborhood? He doesn't live around here, does he?"

"No. At least, I don't think he does. I think he lives in Mayville."

When I was trying to determine who had killed Isabel, I had sat across the street from the Cantonos' house a few times. It's possible they had moved, but I hadn't heard anything. Marcus lived in Reed Hill. He had purchased a home in one of the newer subdivisions; however, Ricky didn't live with him. Ricky, his younger brother Mike, and a couple of cousins had their own place. The only reason I knew that was because Marcus had told me his mother had worried about leaving the boys, her grandsons, alone when she moved in with Marcus.

"Should we follow him?" Myra asked.

I glanced at her. She had a slight smile on her face and a twinkle in her eye. I laughed softly. "I don't think we can catch him. Besides, I want to see if Jose is home."

Jose's house was the fourth one down. I pulled up to the front and parked. It was dark with no signs of life. There was no car in the driveway, although he did have a garage so the car could be parked inside.

"Doesn't look like anyone's home," Myra commented.

"No, but I'm going to check anyway."

We got out and walked to the front door. I reached out to ring the bell when I saw the door was slightly open. A strange feeling of déjà vu came over me, and a heavy weight settled in my stomach. I pushed the door open. It swung out silently. I looked over at Myra. She nodded once so I stepped inside.

The smell hit me first. It was unlike anything I had ever smelled before, but my mind knew what I would find.

"Call 911," I said softly to Myra.

She caught her breath and then quickly backed away. I reached for the wall and felt around for the light switch. The lights flickered on, illuminating the room. I was in a small hallway. A short way down, there were two doorways. I walked a few steps and looked to the left. Jose was lying in the middle of the living room floor. He was wearing only a pair of jeans, no shirt, no shoes, as if he was home for the evening. He had been beaten. Bruises covered his face and chest. And his head was at an odd angle, just like Donnie.

I closed my eyes a moment. Poor Jose. He had been an odd little man, but I hated that he was dead. I backed up and walked outside to join Myra. She was still on the phone with the police.

"Yes," she said. "2438 River Street." She looked at me. I nodded so she added, "We think there's been another murder."

The police arrived quickly, two officers I didn't know. I told them what I found, and Myra and I returned to my car to wait. Griggs and Megan arrived soon after that. They both looked over at us but continued into the house. A few other officers, along with the ME, arrived while we waited.

About twenty minutes later, Griggs and Megan came out.

Griggs motioned to us. Myra and I got out of the car and joined them on the driveway. They both just looked at me so I took a deep breath and started the tale.

"I got Jose's address from Jenny this afternoon. I wanted to see if he had come home yet. After work, Myra and I drove over here. When we got to the front door, it was open. I went in and found Jose. I touched the door, the wall near the light switch, and walked down the hallway. That's it."

"Did you see anything inside?" Megan asked. I shook my head. "Anyone drive by or out for a walk?"

Myra and I exchanged a glance. "Ricky Cantono drove by on a motorcycle."

Griggs and Megan both perked up at that. "You're sure it was Ricky?" Griggs asked.

"Yes."

"Was he coming from here?"

"I don't know. We were at the corner. Just before I turned onto River Street, he flew by on his bike. I could see his face under the streetlight. But I don't know if he was at Jose's or just in the neighborhood."

"We'll check it out. Jose has been dead for close to twenty-four hours, but the door was intact when we came by yesterday. He must have been killed sometime last night."

"So Ricky didn't kill him." I breathed a sigh of relief. I didn't think much of Ricky, but I knew Marcus cared for him.

"Unless he was coming back to the scene of the crime for some reason."

"Why would he do that?"

"Who knows? All I know at this point is we need to talk to Ricky Cantono."

"What now?" I asked.

"You two go home," Griggs said sharply. "I'm going to have a patrol car follow you. They'll be parked outside all night."

"Do you think we're in danger?" Myra asked.

"I think there's a murderer running around. It's best not to take any chances."

We drove to Myra's slowly, both of us lost in our thoughts. The presence of the police car in my rearview mirror was comforting but frightening at the same time. The thought that someone might come after us seemed more real now.

"I'm sorry I got you into this," I said to Myra when we arrived at her house.

"You didn't get me into anything. I wouldn't have been with you if it wasn't because of my ex-husband. That's on me."

"No," I said. "That's on him."

"Either way. It's not your fault. Do you think the same person who killed Donnie murdered Jose?"

Myra hadn't seen either body. For that I was glad. But the way they were both laying made me think they had been killed the same way.

"I do," I told her. "They both looked like someone had broken their neck."

Myra shuddered. "That's horrible."

Before I went to bed, I placed another call to Marcus. He didn't answer this time either. I left him another message, telling him about Jose. I also suggested he might want to hire Ricky a lawyer.

CHAPTER 19

The next morning, Myra and I arrived at the store early. The day had dawned clear and sunny. All the rain from the previous couple of days was gone. The news of Jose's death had made the evening news so I knew we would be busy, but my first visitor of the day was a surprise. Just before we opened, Jenny knocked on the back door.

"Hi, Jenny."

"Leah."

She looked unhappy. She came in and sat in the chair across from my desk. I sat down beside her.

"Are you okay?" I asked.

"I guess. Jose and I weren't friends, but he was a good employee."

"I'm sorry."

"Thanks. I told you yesterday that most of the equipment he used belonged to Gemstones, but he had a few items that belonged to him personally. He kept those in a locked cabinet under his workbench." She took a deep breath. "I had a locksmith open it this morning, and I found this."

She handed me a single sheet of paper. On it was a sketch of my great-grandmother's ring, along with the dimensions. My shoulders slumped. For some reason, I had been holding out hope that Jose was not involved.

"He had a copy of the sketch," I said softly. Jenny nodded. "The police need to know about this."

"I know. I've already called them. Someone's going to come by and get the contents of the cabinet and the sketch." I started to hand her the paper when she shook her head. "That's for you. I made you a copy."

"Jenny…"

"I knew you would want it. Jose obviously got into something he shouldn't have, but I don't think he was a bad person." She paused. "I spoke to his parents."

That had to have been unpleasant. Jenny was normally quiet and restrained. Being pregnant had made her more emotional, and she had a hard time dealing with it.

"How are they doing?" I asked her.

"As well as could be expected, I guess." She smiled slightly. "What a stupid phrase. How can anyone be okay when their child has been murdered?"

"Did they say anything about what Jose has been doing?"

"No. I think they're in shock. They want answers. So does Daniel."

"Daniel?"

"Yes, they were friends."

"Daniel Thompson?" She nodded. Daniel is the owner of Thompson's Rare Books. He is a grumpy old man who doesn't like anyone. He and I have developed an odd relationship. I secretly love the man, and he tolerates me. I feed his sweet tooth, and he lets me browse through his books.

"He's really upset," Jenny said. "It even showed."

Daniel is not the touchy-feely type. His default attitude is cranky. The fact that Jenny could tell he was upset was unusual. I hadn't realized that he and Jose had been friends. Thinking back, I remembered seeing Jose in front of the bookstore from time to time, but Gemstones and Thompson's Rare Books are side by side so I had always assumed Jose was going to or from work.

"It really bothers me that he's dead." Jenny laid her hand

on her swollen belly as if protecting her unborn child. "It scares me that people can kill so easily."

"Whoever did this won't get away with it," I told her. "The police will find the killer."

"Or you will," she said with a smile.

"Jenny, I'm not really involved. I mean…I'm not supposed to be involved."

She just smiled again. "I need to get back to the store. I'll let you know if I hear anything."

After she left, my phone rang. It was Marcus finally returning my calls. I was still in the back room and was glad for the privacy because his voice was cold and hard.

"What the hell were you doing following my nephew?"

I have never heard Marcus yell, and he didn't yell now, but his voice shook me. The first time I had seen him, I knew he was dangerous. I had grown comfortable with him, believing we were friends. That was obviously a mistake. He frightened me, but I refused to be intimidated.

"I'm sorry, Marcus," I said softly, "but we both know Ricky knows more than he's telling us. He's involved with this."

"He's gone, Leah." His voice had softened and was laced with despair and perhaps a little fear.

"What do you mean he's gone?"

"Yesterday was crazy. The restaurant's scheduled to open next week, and we've had so many problems..." He stopped a moment. "I didn't get your message until almost seven. I went to talk to him, but he was already gone. Mike said he had come home in a panic. Ricky grabbed some clothes, took all the cash the other boys had, and took off. The police arrived a few minutes later, saying Jose Alvera was dead, and Ricky had been seen in the area."

I felt a little guilty about that, but there was nothing I could do. I had seen him driving down River Street.

"Jose was killed Wednesday night, but Ricky was on his street last night."

"You saw him?" he asked sharply.

Oops. Apparently, no one had told Marcus that I was the

one who had reported Ricky to the cops. "I saw him driving like a bat out of hell on his motorcycle down River Street."

"Damn it, Leah," he growled. I said nothing. His voice was calmer when he spoke again. "I spent half the night looking for him."

"It doesn't look good that he fled, Marcus. The police will think he's guilty."

"He didn't kill anyone." The complete conviction in his voice convinced me. The amount of time I had spent with Marcus could be counted in hours instead of days, but I trusted him. I couldn't say why, I just know I did.

"Okay."

"Okay?"

"Yeah. If you say he didn't kill anyone, I believe you."

There was a long pause before he said, "Thank you."

"But he *is* involved with this, Marcus. If he's not the killer, then he might well be the next victim. You need to find him and convince him to turn himself in. He'll be safer in jail."

"I'll do what I can." There was another pause. This one shorter. "Thanks for believing me, Leah."

"Sure, we're friends, right?" I hoped he would agree.

"Yes, but…"

"But, what?"

"People like you don't usually believe people like me."

"What the hell is that supposed to mean?"

He chuckled, finally sounding more like himself. "Think about it. Will you tell Chief Griggs what I said? He won't believe me, but he might be persuaded to believe you."

"I wouldn't count on that," I replied. Griggs didn't seem to like any of the Cantonos. "But I'll tell him."

"Tell him on your date. He'll be more susceptible then."

"How'd you know about our date?"

"I think you'll have fun tonight, Leah," he said as he hung up. I shook my head at that odd statement.

Glancing at the clock, I saw that it was five minutes before ten. Kara arrived to help Myra open the store so I had time to make a visit to Daniel. I quickly walked over to Nora's Bakery to pick up his favorite pastry.

Not long after we opened Scents and Sensibility, I discovered Daniel's secret vice. He loves cream cheese empanadas. His wife used to make them for him before she passed away. Daniel refuses to shop in any of the stores downtown so he never ventures into Nora's, but they make wonderful empanadas.

After buying the pastries, I walked back past Scents and Sensibility and turned left onto Main. Thompson's Rare Books is three stores down. I arrived there two minutes after ten, and as I knew it would be, the store was open. Daniel always opens exactly at ten and closes exactly at six. I have actually seen him shoo people out of his store so that he could lock up on time.

The store itself is dark and musty. It's not a large shop, but bookshelves line the walls and aisles. The books are mostly first editions or books that are out of print. They are all rare and expensive. I can't afford to shop there often, but I love browsing the shelves.

Daniel has enough personal income to not need to work and has been known to refuse to sell a book to someone he doesn't think is worthy. He is a wonderful, weird old man. He barely looked up when I walked in.

"Hello, Daniel," I said as I sat the bag of pastries on the counter in front of him. I received a grunt in reply. He glanced at the bag but didn't reach for it. Normally, he pounced on it the moment I sat it down. My heart went out to him. He really was upset.

"Jenny told me you and Jose were friends. I'm sorry for your loss." It was the polite thing to say, the correct thing to say, but it felt hollow. His eyes met mine, and I saw something flash in them briefly. Something I couldn't identify. He looked away.

"You involved?" he asked me.

"No, of cou…" He looked at me again. This time I identified the look in his eyes. It was anger. I swallowed and then nodded. "Yeah, I am."

"So what do you want?"

"Did you know what Jose was doing? Did he say anything?"

"The kid was worried," Daniel said. "Something was bothering him. He didn't say much, but I could tell."

"When was this?"

"Monday afternoon. He stopped by but didn't stay long. I think he wanted to ask me something but couldn't bring himself to do so. I didn't push." Daniel paused. He fiddled with the book lying on the counter. "I shoulda pushed."

"Daniel…"

"What else?" he asked abruptly. I didn't take it personally. Daniel was always abrupt, and I could tell he was hurting. He and Jose must have really bonded.

"What did you and Jose talk about?"

"Books, mostly. He didn't talk much."

"Neither do you," I said with a sad smile.

"Nope."

"Daniel, Jose had a copy of a sketch of a ring that belonged to my great-grandmother. The ring was designed by my great-grandfather—her husband. We thought all his sketches were lost. Donnie, the kid who was murdered last week, had a replica of the ring hidden in his jacket. Three days later, someone broke into my apartment. The police think that the killer is after the ring. Did Jose say anything about that?"

"No," Daniel said slowly. "You think that he was trying to make another ring?"

"Probably. I overheard him and Ricky Cantono discussing a ring. I think someone hired Jose to reproduce my ring."

"The Cantonos are involved with this?"

I told Daniel everything I had learned, including the fact that Ricky Cantono was missing. Marcus probably wouldn't be happy about it, but Daniel had a right to know. I did my best to convince him that Ricky did not kill Jose. The last thing I needed was for the old man to try to avenge his friend. When the Cantonos threatened me back in December, Daniel had shown up with a shotgun. His hands hadn't been too steady. If he went after Ricky, someone would get hurt.

"Why would someone want a copy of your ring?" Daniel asked when I had finished.

"I have absolutely no idea."

"They after you?"

"No…well, I doubt it."

"Where's your gun?" he snapped.

"In my purse, back at the store."

"Keep it with you, you twit."

I suppressed a smile. "Yes, sir. If you remember anything Jose might have said, let me know."

I had started walking toward the door when Daniel called my name. He didn't say my name often. He usually just grunted at me. I turned around. He walked out from behind the counter and came over to me. He is just a little taller than I am so he could look me directly in the eyes.

"You'll find out who did this to Jose?" he asked.

"I'll do my best," I replied. I was in so much trouble. The police would not be happy about my promise, but there was nothing I wouldn't do to remove that sad look from the old man's face. "I promise, Daniel. I'll do my best."

He nodded once. "You gonna buy anything?"

"Nope," I said, inwardly smiling at his question. It was one he asked me every time I came in.

"Then what are you still doing here?" He walked back to the counter.

"Leaving now, Daniel." I turned and opened the door. Just as I was stepping out, I heard the rustle of the paper bag full of pastries. I shut the door softly behind me and grinned. He was going to be okay.

On the way back to the store, I received a call from Gabe asking if I could meet him and Olivia for lunch. We made arrangements to meet at the Reed Hill Café on the square at one. I hadn't been gone long, but when I arrived at Scents and Sensibility, we had several customers. One of them wanted four box sets of our Vanilla Vine product. When I went to the back to pull them, I found David Reddish playing with Harry. David stops by the store about once a week, but I was surprised to see him as I hadn't seen him come in.

"When did you get here?" I asked.

"A few minutes ago. Myra said you had gone to talk to Daniel. Did you learn anything?"

I told David what Daniel had said. David wasn't in charge of this investigation, but I was sure Griggs was keeping him in the loop. Megan was still learning the ropes, and they probably needed all the help they could get. David was an excellent police officer. He listened to what I said and promised to pass along the information. It really wasn't anything new. We already knew Jose was involved. Daniel had just confirmed it.

Myra and I hadn't heard anything from Leon so I asked Reddish about that. I was a little concerned about leaving her alone when I went out with Griggs. David told me that Leon was staying at the Main Street Inn, and they were watching him as much as they could. The police didn't have the manpower to follow him 24/7, but a patrol car drove by regularly. That didn't ease my concerns as Leon could easily slip out when no one was around. The Main Street Inn catered to the temporarily displaced. It wasn't in the best part of town. No one would notice or care about what Leon was doing.

I was trying to decide what to do about Myra when David solved the problem for me. He stated, somewhat casually, that he would stop by Myra's this evening as he knew I would be out with the chief. Apparently the whole town knew I had a date with Griggs.

CHAPTER 20

Lunch with Gabe and Olivia was a little awkward. I often have lunch with Olivia and occasionally with Gabe but seldom with both of them at the same time. They are my two best friends so I see them often. We are just usually surrounded by their children. It didn't take me long to realize they wanted something.

"Okay, out with it," I finally said after we had been seated at the table for about twenty minutes. Our food had arrived, and they were still making small talk.

Gabe laid down his fork, looked at Olivia, and grinned. "Told ya."

Olivia rolled her eyes and shook her head. She picked up a piece of bread from the basket on the table and started buttering it. "Don't look so smug. I never doubted she would know we wanted something. I just said she wouldn't know what it was."

They both looked expectantly at me. I racked my brain, trying to think. What could they possibly want from me? The only odd thing that had happened recently was the issue with Aaron. I had already found out what he was doing. What could be left? Then it dawned on me.

"No," I said quickly. "No way. I'm not going to be

involved with his punishment. He already hates me."

"He doesn't hate you, Leah," Gabe said. "He's just angry."

"He has reason. I betrayed him."

"Leah," Olivia said. "You didn't betray him. He knows I asked you to see if you could find out what he was doing. He's really mad at me and Gabe. That's why we are hoping you can help us."

I sighed. "What do you want me to do?"

"He's already been grounded, and he has to use his allowance to pay for the fence slats," Gabe replied. "We spoke with the builder. They were going to throw them away so it wasn't a problem, but Aaron didn't know that. He's been moping around the house because he can't go anywhere."

"We don't want him to think he's getting away with anything," Olivia added, "but we think he's learned his lesson. What we want is to make him do something that appears to be a punishment but will actually be fun for him."

"What'd you have in mind?"

"You're staying with Myra, right?" Gabe asked. I nodded. "She has horses, doesn't she?"

"Yes," I said with a grin.

"Think she could use someone to help clean out the stalls?"

"I think she might. And then the horses will need exercise."

"Exactly," Olivia said. "He loves to ride."

"When do you want this to happen?"

Gabe and Olivia exchanged a look. "We're hoping tomorrow."

Olivia raised her hand before I could respond. "He's bored. It can't be Sunday because that's our monthly lunch."

On the first Sunday of each month, Gabe and Olivia invite friends and family to their house for lunch. It's a lively affair. We eat, watch a game or movie, and talk. They could cancel it, but a lot of people, including me, look forward to it.

"But the store…Saturday is our busiest day."

"I know you are short-handed," Olivia said quickly. "Gabe will bring Aaron over at eight. I'll open the store with Kara. Carla will come in for a few hours as well. You and Myra can come in later in the day."

Olivia didn't work in the store often, but she shadowed me for a week every year and worked the floor every couple of months. Her goal was to be able to understand everything in case I was ever unable to work. Carla is Gabe's mother, and she loves the store. She mostly gossips, but she's familiar with all the products. She could certainly talk to the customers and send them in the right direction. Kara and Olivia could handle the rest.

"Alright," I replied. "I'll talk to Myra, but I think it should be okay."

"Good," Olivia said. "We appreciate it."

The conversation turned to the murders. I updated Gabe and Olivia on everything I had learned since I last spoke with them. It was nice to talk to people I knew so well and who knew me. I could throw out any silly idea for discussion.

We narrowed down the list of suspects to three. Sean Walters, Ricky Cantono, and Leon Hollins. I decided to eliminate Sean or at least put him at the bottom of the list. Other than his connection to Ricky and Albert's designs, there was nothing to link him to Donnie or the ring. And as far as I knew, he and Jose didn't know each other at all.

Ricky Cantono was a different story. Donnie and Jose were both linked to Ricky. I knew Ricky was selling drugs, but I truly hoped that he wasn't a murderer. Marcus loved his nephew. With Damian in jail, Marcus was the boys' only role model. Maybe with a little time, Marcus could convince them to give up their life of crime. He had said that Ricky didn't kill anyone, and I believed him. Unfortunately, Marcus could be wrong. Ricky was involved. He might not have killed anyone, but he had known Donnie, bribed Sean into creating the rose, and threatened Jose about the ring. For Marcus's sake, I wanted to eliminate Ricky. I just couldn't.

Leon Hollins was at the top of my list. He was big enough and strong enough to break the victims' necks, and he had the military training. He had broken into my apartment, presumably to steal the ring and the rose. Myra had said he had a temper, and I had seen that first hand. Two people had seen him talking to Jose so there was a connection there. The problem was there was no connection between Donnie and Leon. It was possible they knew each other, but if the police had discovered it, they hadn't told me. How had Leon even learned about the ring and the rose in the first place?

"Well, that didn't help much," I said in disgust.

"It's not your job to solve this, Leah," Gabe said.

"I know. I just want to know."

"Of course you do," Olivia said. "And the police will find the killer. Now, what are you wearing on your date tonight?"

"Liv," Gabe said in a pleading voice. He is often subjected to our girl talk. Most of the time, he handles it well, but he's always uncomfortable when we talk about me dating. Clothes, makeup, hair, and even sappy movies, he's okay with, but when we talk guys, he gets this weird look on his face and closes up. I'm too much like a sister to him.

"Oh hush," Olivia told him. "Eat your lunch and let us talk."

"I think I'm done," he said, pushing his chair back. "I'm going to walk around. I'll meet you back at Scents and Sensibility."

We watched him quickly walk out the door. Olivia started to giggle. "He's such a guy."

"Which you love about him," I said with a smile.

"True. It *is* one of his most attractive qualities."

"That he's a guy?" I said with a laugh.

"Yeah." She grinned. "So what are you going to wear?"

"I don't know. I don't know where we're going."

"He didn't tell you where he was taking you?"

"No," I replied. "He just said he would pick me up at seven. I've been assuming this is a date, but he never actually said that either."

"Oh, it's a date," Olivia said.

"What makes you so sure?"

"He ran it by Gabe."

"What?" I yelped. "He did what?"

"Lower your voice. He's right over there."

Olivia nodded slightly to the right. I turned in my seat a little and saw Griggs sitting at a nearby table with Ben Parker, Reed Hill's current mayor. My heart started to flutter before I took a deep breath. The man was going to give me a heart attack. I turned back to Olivia.

"How long has he been there?"

"Since we sat down. They must have gotten seated right before we did."

"Whatever. What's this about him running our date by Gabe?"

Olivia shrugged and took a drink of tea. "He just casually mentioned to Gabe that he was going to ask you out. Gabe said he thought Alex was making sure we didn't have a problem with it. He didn't exactly ask permission, but he gave Gabe an opportunity to object."

"So if Gabe objected, he wouldn't have asked me out?" I wasn't happy with that notion. If Griggs needed permission to ask me out, maybe he wasn't the man I thought he was.

"Don't do this, Leah," Olivia said with a sigh.

"Do what?"

"Invent excuses. You always think of some reason why the guy isn't the right one."

"I don't!" I said emphatically. "I just don't want to go out with someone who has to ask permission like we were still in high school. I'm thirty-five years old, not fifteen."

An exasperated look crossed Olivia's face. She placed her napkin down on the table, leaned forward, and looked me directly in the eyes. "Stop it! It wasn't like that at all, and you know it. I don't believe for a minute that he wouldn't have asked you out if Gabe had objected. He was just verifying that your friends, the people who love you, knew what was going on."

"Maybe," I said reluctantly.

Olivia shook her head. "You are such…"

"Hello, ladies."

Griggs's deep smoky voice came from directly behind me.

He moved closer and was soon standing beside the table. The mayor was standing next to him. I murmured something incoherent, but Olivia smiled brightly and greeted them. I sat there silently while they chatted. Mayor Parker knows the Westons well. He and I run into each other occasionally at one of the city functions, but I seldom speak to him. I don't like him. He is a womanizer and a first-class jerk. Unfortunately, he is also a really good mayor. He has brought a lot of commerce to the area and improved the streets and public parks. I had voted for him and probably will again, but I don't have to like him.

The mayor finished speaking with Olivia and turned to me. He gave me his smarmy smile. "Hello, Leah."

"Mr. Mayor."

"Try not to find any more bodies. It's bad for business," he said with a booming laugh. He was a large man, a little thick around the waist, big, strong arms, and a beefy complexion.

"I'll do my best," I replied dryly.

Griggs had stepped back so that he was standing just behind the mayor. His mouth twitched at my tone. He had to work to keep from laughing.

"Well, I need to be on my way," the mayor said. "We need to do lunch again soon, Chief."

"I look forward to it," Griggs answered.

"Ladies." Parker nodded at us. We all watched him make his way across the restaurant. He stopped at a couple of tables before walking out the door.

"The mayor is one-of-a-kind," Griggs said, as he pulled out the chair next to me.

"He's an ass," I replied. Olivia laughed and Griggs chuckled.

"So he's a one-of-a-kind ass," Griggs added as he sat down.

"Wasn't he a marine?" I asked.

"I think so," Griggs replied with a puzzled look. "Why?"

"I want to add him to my list of suspects. He's big enough and has military training. Surely, that's got to count for something."

Griggs smiled. "I don't think the mayor is killing people in Reed Hill City Park, but I'll keep it in mind."

"He's an ass. Maybe that can count as well." I looked at Griggs. He was dressed in his usual suit and tie. I could see his badge and gun holster on his belt. He looked relaxed sitting at our table. "You're working today, right?"

"Yes, but I'm not going to arrest the mayor for you."

"Then what good are you?"

"Oh," he said, leaning back in the chair with a wicked grin. "I bet we can think of something."

I had to will the blush away. I needed to stop sparring with Griggs. I could never win. Olivia had her head down, studying her dessert, but I could see the smile lurking. Before I could come up with a response, Griggs let me off the hook.

"Gabe left in a hurry. What did you ladies do to chase him off?"

Olivia took the last bite of her dessert before answering. "We were discussing your date with Leah."

"Really?"

He looked back and forth at us. I shrugged and gave him an enigmatic smile. I wasn't about to touch that one; however, Olivia jumped right in.

"I was asking her what she was going to wear," she said, pointing her fork at Griggs. "You didn't tell Leah where you were going. Not fair, Alex. Not fair at all."

He smiled, the indentation deepened, and my toes curled. Damn! I quietly took a deep breath and looked away.

"Sorry," he said. "I should've discussed it with you."

Shrugging again, I tried to sound nonchalant. "You like throwing out a line and walking away."

Silence descended on the table for a moment before Griggs burst out laughing. "I guess I do like doing that. The look on your face is always priceless."

I narrowed my eyes and glared at him. He smiled and then raised his hands in surrender. Still chuckling, he sat forward and leaned on the table.

"We have an invitation to the private opening for Bella's."

"What?" I screeched. Bella's was Marcus's new restaurant. I hadn't heard anything about a private opening.

"We're going too," Olivia said with a smile.

Stunned, I stared at her a moment, trying to will away the pain. Marcus had invited Griggs, a police officer, when the Cantonos avoided the police at all costs, and Gabe and Olivia, who I don't think he had ever even met. Why hadn't he invited me?

"I thought you would enjoy it," Griggs said softly, "but if you don't want to go, we can do something else."

"No," I said, quickly hiding the hurt. "That sounds fun. I've been looking forward to eating there."

"If you're sure…"

"I'm sure. You know I love Italian."

We chatted a few more minutes. I don't think Griggs knew anything was wrong, but I hadn't fooled Olivia. We paid our bill and left. Griggs headed back to the station, and Olivia and I walked back to Scents and Sensibility. She didn't question me, although I knew she wanted to. Gabe was waiting for us when we arrived. He and Olivia left a few minutes later after confirming with Myra that Aaron could help with the horses. And I was left alone with my thoughts.

CHAPTER 21

The rest of the day passed slowly. We were busy and had a steady stream of customers, but I couldn't keep my mind off the upcoming evening. Time seemed to crawl. I was surprised at how hurt I was that Marcus hadn't invited me personally to his event. I picked up the phone a number of times to call him but never followed through. Each time I thought I had a handle on my relationship with him, something happened to throw me off.

Late that afternoon, I took a few minutes to go through my notes on Donnie's murder. Lunch with Gabe and Olivia had helped to clarify some things in my mind, but there were a lot of unanswered questions. One was concerning the Cantono family. Had Ricky taken over the drug dealing business from his father? Marcus seemed determined to bring his family to the legitimate side of the law. I hoped he could succeed.

Another question was how my great-grandmother's ring and wooden rose fit into all of this. I still didn't see how either item could lead to murder. Nonetheless, the connection was definitely there.

The number of people who originally knew about the two items was small. Donnie learned about the ring from Arthur's sketches, but where did he learn about the wooden rose? He also had to have told Ricky. How many others did he tell? Several other people could be involved. The problem was I had no clue how to determine who they might be.

I had asked Griggs at lunch if there was any new information on Jose. He had confirmed that Jose had been killed in the same manner as Donnie. Jose had died sometime late Wednesday evening after the police had gone by his house and Leon Hollins had been released from jail. Griggs thought that Jose had left Gemstones after I arrived to speak with Jenny because he believed I suspected something, and that he then contacted the killer either to report in or try to get out. The killer then arranged to meet with Jose and murdered him. It bothered me that my actions might have caused Jose's death, even indirectly, but it made me even more determined to make sure the murderer was punished.

By the time six o'clock came around, I was a bundle of nerves. Kara and Myra sent me home, saying they would stay and clean up. I left for my apartment to get ready. Although I was staying with Myra, I had told Griggs to pick me up at my place. There was no reason to drive out to her farm just to turn around and drive back into town. The apartment felt empty without Harry and Pandora, and without the distractions, I was ready twenty minutes early.

Pacing didn't help so I turned on the radio. It didn't distract me much, but at least it gave me something to listen to while I paced. The station had a brief news segment ten minutes before the hour every hour. At ten to seven, I learned that Jose was the oldest of four children and had been helping pay for his siblings' college education. His family was devastated. Tears filled my eyes, and I finally stopped pacing.

Donnie had been a relative, but I hadn't known him at all. Wade and his father didn't seem to mourn him much which was sad but had allowed me to distance myself. Jose was different. I knew him. I had always thought he was a little odd, yet he had been, at least somewhat, part of my life. I saw him once or twice a week. There were people, like Daniel, who would miss him. For the first time, I wished I had known him better.

There was a knock on my door at exactly seven o'clock. I smoothed down my skirt and went to answer it. I hadn't been this nervous about a date since my high school prom. I don't date a lot, but I have had my share of boyfriends. There was something about Griggs that just felt more—more intense, more powerful, more real. I was falling hard and fast and that scared me.

When I opened the door, he was standing there dressed in a suit and looking delicious. His eyes roamed my face for a moment before drifting down my entire body and back up. He did that a lot. It never failed to take my breath away. He gave me a slow, seductive smile, and I had to remind myself to breathe.

"You look great," he said.

"Thanks. You, too." I was pleased to hear my voice sounded normal. "You want to come in?"

"Not now," he replied with another smile. "If you're ready, we should go."

"Sure." I gathered my purse. This was a smaller one than the ones I usually carry. It was more of an evening clutch, but it, too, had an embedded holster for a gun. I didn't bring my gun though. I figured that as long as I was with Griggs there wasn't a need.

As we drove toward the restaurant, I began to relax. Griggs and I talked briefly about happenings around town. We kept the conversation light avoiding the murders or anything too serious. It only took about ten minutes to arrive.

Bella's is located on the west side of town near the main highway that leads into Dallas. It's a good location as it will attract people from Reed Hill but is also visible from the highway which would pull in people driving through town.

There were several cars in the parking lot and when we walked through the door, I could see four or five tables were already occupied. Marcus appeared in front of us before I had a chance to really look around.

"Leah," he said. "You look lovely."

"Thanks."

"Griggs." Marcus offered his hand.

"Cantono." They shook briefly while I tried not to roll my eyes. The posturing was getting old.

"Thanks for bringing her," Marcus said.

"That was the agreement," Griggs replied.

"What? What agreement?"

Marcus turned to me and smiled. My heartbeat sped up just a little even as I felt a frown forming on my face.

"Mike," Marcus called. His nephew walked over. Mike Cantono looks a little bit like his uncle. Same coloring and build. He's better-looking than his older brother Ricky, but nowhere near as handsome as Marcus. The last time I had seen Mike, he had been threatening me with a knife. Now he looked like a young, neatly dressed waiter.

"Please show Chief Griggs to the Westons' table," Marcus told him. He turned to Griggs. "I'll return her to you in a few minutes."

"I'm not a package," I muttered. I heard Griggs chuckle as he followed Mike across the restaurant.

Marcus took my arm and led me into the bar area. It was a beautiful room with several tables and chairs and a long bar at the back. Behind the bar, from floor to ceiling, were two large wine racks. Every slot was filled.

"This is our wine bar," Marcus said. "We'll serve other alcohol, but wine will be our specialty."

"It's gorgeous. What agreement?"

He laughed. "Earlier this week, I decided to host a private opening for some of the more prominent members of our town. I had fully intended to invite you as my date. However, the chief warned me off."

I stared at him in shock. I didn't know whether to be flattered or insulted. "He did what?"

"Well, maybe I'm exaggerating a little. He was at the gym when I invited your friend Gabe. I mentioned that I would be inviting you, and that I hoped they would come so that you could sit with them while I was busy taking care of my guests.

Griggs then informed me that he had plans with you for tonight."

"Hmm," I said. As far as I could determine, that conversation should have happened before Griggs had asked me out.

Marcus pulled on the cuffs of his shirt under the sleeves of his suit jacket. "Being the gentleman that I am and knowing you have a crush on him, I…"

"I don't have a crush on him!" I interjected quickly. Marcus just looked at me, a slight smile dancing around his mouth. Finally, I rolled my eyes. "Okay, maybe a small crush."

"So I invited him to the opening with the agreement that he bring you." Humor still lined his voice, but he managed to say it with a straight face.

My brain processed all the information, and I couldn't think of a reason to be upset. Marcus had intended to invite me, which soothed my hurt feelings. Griggs had already said he was planning to follow up on the kiss we shared. And my friends were here to enjoy the evening with me.

"Besides," Marcus said with a twinkle in his eyes, "having the chief of police eat at my restaurant will lend legitimacy to my business."

I reached out and hit him. He laughed again. "Come on, I'll show you to your table."

When we reached the doorway, I stopped again. "Marcus, have you heard from Ricky?"

A shadow crossed his face. He shook his head. "Not directly. He called Mike this afternoon but wouldn't tell him where he was. Mike told him to contact me, but Ricky said he needed to do something first."

"What?" I asked.

"He wouldn't say. He simply told Mike not to worry and to tell me to stop looking for him."

"And did you?"

Marcus's eyes grew distant. "For now."

"I hope he's okay," I whispered softly.

"Me, too."

The next two hours were spent talking, laughing, and eating. The food was delicious and the wine superb. Gabe, Olivia, and I spend a lot of time together so the conversation flowed freely. Griggs had no trouble joining in, and my friends made sure to include him. In some ways, they knew Alex better than I did as they had both spent time with him during city council events. It was the most relaxed and comfortable I had ever seen him. Of course, all the times I had been around him before he was trying to solve a murder. There was no murder talk that night.

People came and went throughout the entire time we were there. I estimated that over fifty people attended the event. Marcus obviously knew what he was doing. The crowd consisted of the most prominent people in town. Not the wealthiest, but the most influential. Besides the four of us, the mayor was in attendance, as were most of the other members of the city council. But Marcus had also invited a couple of reporters, the local head of the theatre association, the owners of several small businesses, and the presidents of two nonprofit organizations. I overheard him offering to donate a dinner for two for their next fundraiser.

Just as the evening was ending, I excused myself to use the restroom. As I stepped back into the hallway to return to the table, I felt someone behind me. When I turned around, I saw Mike Cantono. I froze a moment. He and I weren't exactly buddies. The last time we had been that close, he was holding a knife and I was pointing a gun at him. I forced myself to relax. He wasn't going to do anything to me in the hallway of his uncle's restaurant. I watched him a minute and realized he looked nervous and uncomfortable.

"Mike," I said. "Everything all right?"

He gave me a slight smile. It made him look cute. He looked away and then back again. "I wanted to say…sorry. You know, for that night."

Marcus had managed to reach at least one of his nephews. Hopefully, Mike was now on the right path. I nodded to him. "Okay."

He grinned suddenly, and I had to smile back. His grin was a lot like his uncle's. He was going to break a few hearts in his time. When he started to walk away, I stopped him. "Mike, have you heard from Ricky?"

Marcus had said that Ricky had called Mike earlier, but I was hoping he had called again. I didn't like Ricky much, but I had a terrible feeling he was in danger.

"Not since this afternoon." I nodded again and started to leave when he made a slight sound. I looked back, but he wouldn't meet my eyes. He bounced the heel of his foot a few times nervously. "He…"

"He what?" I asked softly. Mike swallowed. I took a step closer. "Mike, did Ricky say something else to you?"

"No, it's just…he has a girl."

"Ricky has a child?" I asked surprised.

"No, no. He has a girlfriend, Vanessa."

I remembered that Griggs had told me that Ricky's alibi for Donnie's murder was that he was with his girlfriend.

"You think Ricky might be with Vanessa?" I asked Mike.

"No," he replied. "See, I…I ain't seen her lately."

"You think she's involved…" A hard knot formed in my stomach as the implications sunk in. "Or that she's missing and being used against Ricky?"

"Look," Mike said. "All I know is there ain't much Ricky wouldn't do for Vanessa."

I leaned against the wall and tilted my head back. My brain worked feverishly trying to sort out my thoughts. Why would the killer use Vanessa? What did Ricky know or have that was so important? I turned back to Mike.

"Does her family know she might be missing?"

"Far as I know, she don't have one."

"Do you know where she lives?"

He gave me her address. "But she ain't there."

"Maybe not, but it's a place to start."

Mike headed to the kitchen, and I returned to our table. Everyone had finished with their meal so we decided to call it a night. I tried to speak with Marcus, but he was tied up with a customer. He gave me a quick smile and thanked us for coming. I decided it would be better to call him later. In the parking lot, Gabe and Olivia said good night, and Griggs and I returned to his car. After he had helped me in, he walked around to his side and got in. Before starting the car, he turned to me and said, "So what did you learn from Mike when you went to the restroom?"

CHAPTER 22

"This isn't how I was hoping the second part of this date would go," Griggs said as he pulled into the Harbor Trailer Park.

"Oh," I replied absently, looking at the numbers on the signs. "What exactly did you expect?"

He turned to me with a mischievous grin and waggled his eyebrows up and down. I started laughing. "Really? On a first date?"

"Hey, a guy can hope."

"It's the fourth one," I said, humor still lining my voice. The trailers in the park were not in the best condition. Most of them were rusted and had peeling paint. The park was small. It had two lanes with trailers on either side. Many of the slots were empty with overgrown grass and weeds. There was even an abandoned bicycle in one of them. It was a depressing place.

After I had recovered from the shock of Griggs asking me what I had learned from Mike at Bella's, I told him what the kid had said. The police had questioned Vanessa briefly to verify Ricky's alibi but nothing more. Griggs reported it to Megan and told her to see what she could find out about the girl. I then convinced him to at least drive by to see if she was at home. He knew that if he didn't, I would have come on my own. He didn't put up much of a fight. I think he was worried about her too.

Vanessa's trailer was one of the smaller ones, but it appeared to be in a little better shape than some of the others. The small yard was neat, and the trailer itself appeared to be clean and recently painted. On the outside anyway. Griggs pulled to a stop, and we got out.

No one answered when we knocked on the door. My worry deepened. I was trying to peer in the small window when the door of the trailer across from Vanessa's opened. A woman stood in the half-open doorway staring at us.

She looked to be in her fifties, but I was betting she was probably younger. Time had not been kind to her. She only had a little gray lining her hair, but her face was thin and haggard. She was wearing an oversized t-shirt and sweatpants and smoking a cigarette, the smoke billowing around her face.

"Whatcha doing?" she asked harshly.

Griggs started toward her. I put a hand on his arm to stop him, leaned over and softly said, "Let me."

He looked at me a moment then nodded. He walked over to the SUV and leaned against it. I took a few steps forward into the light spilling from her doorway.

"We're looking for Vanessa."

"Why?"

"We're worried about her. Her boyfriend's mixed up with some bad people, and we think she might be in trouble."

The woman studied me a moment. "You a cop?"

"No," I answered honestly. I didn't want to scare her off, but I wasn't going to lie so I didn't mention anything about Griggs. Her eyes flickered to him before coming back to land on me. She didn't say anything. I took another step closer. "Have you seen her lately?"

"No." The woman took a drag from her cigarette. "Not since Monday."

"Is that normal? Is she gone a lot?"

"Nah. That girl's responsible. Always at work. Always

helping others. Nothing like her mother."

"Is her mother around? Maybe someone we can talk to or who could let us in to look around?"

"Her mom died last year." I waited for her to continue, but that seemed to be the end of the conversation. I nodded once and turned away. I was halfway between her door and the SUV when she stopped me. "You really think Vanessa's in trouble?"

Turning around, I looked at the woman more closely. She was worried too. Taking a deep breath, I leveled with her. "Ricky's involved with something he shouldn't be. So, yes, I think she's in trouble."

The woman's eyes flicked to Griggs one more time. She raised her chin, indicating him. "He a cop?"

"Yes."

"Don't like cops." There was a long pause. She tossed the cigarette on the small step and crushed it out with her foot. "I got a key. I'll get it."

Griggs walked over to me when she went back inside. "It might be best if I wait in the car. She didn't seem too friendly."

"She doesn't like cops," I told him. He laughed softly. The sound sent a shiver down my spine—in a good way. The trailer door reopened. Griggs walked away. I heard the car door open and close behind me. The woman came down the stairs and together we walked over to Vanessa's trailer.

"I'm Leah by the way," I said.

"Dee."

"Nice to meet you."

Dee just grunted. She opened the door and motioned me in. The place looked even smaller inside, but everything was neat and tidy. It was essentially one room. There was a curtain that could be pulled across to section off the bed from the rest of the trailer, but it was open. The bed was made and nothing appeared out of place. I walked past the tiny bathroom and over to the closet near the bed. Opening the door revealed two dresses, a few shirts, and a couple of pairs of slacks. I turned back to Dee.

"Can you tell if anything's missing? Maybe she packed a

bag?"

Dee joined me at the closet. She shook her head. "Can't say for sure, but she didn't have a lot of clothes. That looks like most of them."

Looking around the trailer, I homed in on the couch. My heart stopped when I saw her purse. Biting my lip, I walked over, picked it up, and looked inside. A wallet, keys, and a few other personal items. When I pulled out the wallet, I heard a slight sound behind me but didn't turn around. Inside were her driver's license and some cash. Sighing, I returned the wallet to the purse. Vanessa did not leave of her own free will.

One last look around did not divulge anything new. I finally looked at Dee. She had her arms wrapped around her stomach, a look of despair on her face. She knew what the purse meant as well as I did. I didn't know what to say to her so I didn't say anything at all. I simply thanked her for her help and left.

Griggs started the car as soon as I got in. The road was one-way so he had to drive down to the end and up the other side. We had only driven a few yards when he spoke. "Well?"

"Nothing looked disturbed, but her purse was there. Wallet, driver's license, keys," I said softly.

Griggs cursed and pulled into the first vacant slot. I sat, staring out the window and listening absently as he called in to the station. What did Ricky know that could cause someone to take Vanessa? It just didn't make any sense.

"I have patrol cars out looking for her. Ross will conduct a background check and see if anything pops. She'll also check with Vanessa's employer. See if she took time off from work or just didn't show."

He backed up the car and drove down the road out of the trailer park. When I didn't say anything, he asked, "You okay?"

"I just have a really bad feeling there's going to be another body."

There was a long pause. "I don't know. Ricky has been agitated but not depressed or sad. If he's smart, and I think he is, he's making sure she's still alive before he agrees to do anything."

"What could they possibly need Ricky for?"

"That's what we need to find out." There was another pause. "Leah, you need to know, we also have to look at Ricky and the other Cantonos."

"You don't think it's the murderer who has Vanessa?"

"I do think it's the murderer who has her, but we wouldn't be doing our job if we didn't look at everyone. Ricky is her boyfriend. That's usually the first place we start. We also need to consider the fact that it could be something else altogether. Unfortunately, people do simply disappear. We'll check all the angles."

I nodded and sat back in the seat. We were driving down Main Street toward the downtown area. There were several other cars on the road. I glanced at the clock on the dashboard and was surprised to find it was only ten thirty. It seemed like it should have been so much later. Griggs was stopped at a light when I heard him murmur, "What the hell is he doing?"

He was looking out the driver's window. I leaned forward to see what had captured his attention. Directly across the street was a small shopping center. It contained a dry cleaner's, a donut shop, and a convenience store. The convenience store was open twenty-four hours and had several cars in the parking lot. The light from the sign made it easy to see the front entryway. A man walked directly in front of the door and headed around the corner onto Oak.

"Is that Leon?" I asked.

"Yes, it is."

"Where's he going?"

"I don't know, but I'm going to find out."

Griggs pulled into the parking lot and turned off the car. He pulled out his gun, checked it, and looked at me. "Stay here. I'll be right back."

"Yeah, right." I opened my door and got out.

"Leah!" I looked back at him still in the car. There was no way I was staying behind. He must have seen the resolve on my face. He let out a frustrated sound but got out of the car as well. He walked over to me. "Stay behind me. And do *exactly* as

I say."

"Okay." I raised my hands and nodded briskly. He muttered something else and started across the lot. I followed close behind.

Griggs still wore his suit jacket, but I was wearing only my dress. I hadn't thought to bring a jacket or sweater with me. It was early March and the weather had warmed, but there was a slight nip in the air. I hoped I wouldn't be too cold. My biggest concern was my shoes. The two-inch heels sounded very loud on the concrete pavement. Once we turned onto Oak, however, the concrete disappeared, and we had to walk on the dead grass on the side of the road. My heels sank into the damp ground, and I resigned myself to another lost pair of shoes.

Leon was nowhere to be seen. I started to say something when Griggs sped up. I hurried to catch up with him. We came to an alleyway. Griggs stopped and peered carefully around the corner. He shook his head and moved forward. We did this two more times. I was just about to give up and return to the car when we finally heard voices.

Griggs pulled me back against the wall and held a finger to his lips. I nodded once. There were two distinct voices, but I couldn't hear the words. I tapped Griggs on the arm, and then tugged my ear when he looked at me. He shook his head no. He couldn't hear them either. He motioned me to stay, then crouched down and looked around the corner before disappearing from sight.

I stood there, heart pounding, straining to hear. The two voices continued, and then suddenly, Griggs's voice cut through the air. "Police! Hands where I can see them."

There was a startled exclamation and a muffled curse. I leaned over and looked around the corner. Griggs was standing in the middle of the alleyway about twenty yards away, gun pointed directly at two men. There was just enough light from the streetlamps that I could see their faces. One was Leon; the other was Ricky Cantono. I didn't know whether to be relieved or alarmed. I walked a few steps into the alley. No one noticed me so I went a little closer.

"Hey," Leon said sharply. "We're just two guys having a chat. We're not doing anything wrong. You can't hold us."

Griggs's jaw clenched. I could see the frustration on his face. He narrowed his eyes and glared at Leon. "Don't push it, Hollins. Ricky here is wanted for questioning in a murder case."

Leon looked at Griggs, then at Ricky, and back at Griggs. He opened his mouth and then closed it again. He took a step forward, hands closed into fists, and I thought he might actually challenge Griggs. I quickly looked around for a weapon, but the alley was empty of anything useful. There was some trash, but unless I wanted to hit him over the head with a paper cup, I was out of luck. Fortunately, it didn't come down to that.

Leon relaxed his fists and stepped back. "Fine, but I'm outta here."

He turned sideways to face Ricky, his back to Griggs. I saw him mouth something before turning away. He stopped again briefly when he saw me, gave me a nasty smile, and swept by in a hurry. I twisted to watch and make sure he left the alley. When I turned back, Griggs had lowered his gun.

"Are you going to come peacefully?"

Ricky nodded. Griggs pulled out his phone and called the station. When he was done, he tossed me his key. "Why don't you wait in the car?"

I wasn't sure I should leave Griggs alone, but he had already lowered his gun and was standing next to Ricky, talking to him. I made my way back to the SUV and settled in to wait. A few minutes later, a patrol car drove by and about ten minutes after that Griggs appeared.

"I need to get to the station so I'm going to take you home. Do you want to go back to your place or Myra's?"

"Mine. I need to get my car."

We drove in silence. I was glad that Ricky was safe. Hopefully, the police could get him to talk. If not, at least the murderer couldn't get to him in jail. I was still worried about

Vanessa, but there was nothing else I could do about it. Megan was looking into her life. Maybe she would find something that would help locate the girl.

Griggs pulled up next to my car. "Are you going up to the apartment?"

"No. I just wanted my car for tomorrow. I'll go straight to Myra's."

He got out and walked me to the car. He checked the backseat and trunk while I watched, trying not to laugh. My car was new because the last one had been totaled when I was run off the road. It was a tiny thing. No grown man could hide in the trunk or backseat.

"It doesn't hurt to be safe," he growled when he saw the humor on my face. I just laughed. He took a step forward and the laughter died. He raised one hand and cupped my cheek. "Sorry about the date."

"Oh, I don't know. It was unique." He smiled. The indentation in his cheek deepened, and I badly wanted to lean forward and kiss it. I resisted because I wasn't sure we were there yet. Instead, I leaned forward and kissed him softly on the lips before saying sheepishly, "I actually had fun."

He threw his head back and laughed. "Of course you did. You got to question a witness, and trail a suspect."

"Don't forget. I got a really nice dinner out of it, too."

"I really need to go," he said. I nodded. He leaned forward and kissed me. "Here's my line to throw out and then walk away. Don't leave town."

I drove the entire way to Myra's with a smile on my face. It was still there when I fell asleep.

CHAPTER 23

"Aunt Leah, I'm done with this one," Aaron called.

I walked over and looked around at the stall. It was nice and tidy. Gabe had dropped Aaron off at eight. We had been working in the barn since then. Myra had found several small jobs that Aaron could do. She only had two horses so it didn't take us long. It was just now nine o'clock.

"Nice job," I said.

Myra walked up next to me and smiled at Aaron. "You do good work. I may have to hire you when you get a little older."

Aaron grinned and stood just a little taller. When he first arrived, he wasn't sure what to expect. Olivia had told him part of his punishment for stealing the fence slats was to help Myra with some chores. He had been a little apprehensive, but as soon as he realized he was going to be working with the horses, he jumped right in. It was hard work, but he loved being around animals.

"Now," Myra said, "the horses need to be exercised. Why don't you go get Maxie? We'll saddle her up, and you and I will go for a ride."

His face lit up, and the grin widened. "Really?"

"Your parents told me that you had to help me with the horses," Myra said in a stern voice. "They need their exercise, and it takes too much time for me to take them out one at a time."

Aaron looked at me. I frowned briefly. "You better get going. Myra and I have to be at the store by noon."

He shot off in a flash. Myra and I laughed softly. I turned to her. "Thanks for doing this. He's having a great time."

"He's been a lot of help," she replied. "I meant it when I said he does good work."

I glanced out the back door of the barn to see Aaron headed to the nearby paddock. We had moved the horses outside while cleaning the barn. Myra had brought Clover back in after Aaron had finished cleaning the first stall, but Maxie was still in the paddock. She was an old mare and very docile. She seldom broke out of a slow trot. The kids loved her, and the feeling appeared to be mutual.

"I'll take him around the pasture. We'll ride over to the Harrisons' and then come back. They don't mind if I use their place. It should take us about an hour, then you and I can get cleaned up and still be at work before it gets busy."

"That sounds good."

"So tell me how the date went. Did you have a good time?" Myra had been asleep when I arrived back at her house so we hadn't had a chance to talk. I quickly filled her in.

"So what was your favorite part?" she asked when I finished. "Questioning that Dee woman or following Leon?"

"You're as bad as Griggs," I said with a huff. "I enjoyed the meal too."

She smiled, but the smile faded quickly. "I don't know what to make of Leon. He always had a temper. He certainly threatened me once or twice, but I didn't expect him to be involved with anything like this."

There was nothing I could say to comfort her. I couldn't imagine how she felt. Leon was a nasty man, but she must have cared for him at some point. They had built a life together, had a child.

"Do you think he killed Donnie and Jose?" she asked softly.

"I don't know, Myra. I hope not."

"I just don't understand it. What do I tell Jill? She loves her dad. He's never done anything criminal before. Why now? What changed?"

"He got tired of waiting for you," said a voice behind us. We both turned around quickly. I stiffened and felt Myra gasped softly.

"Hello, cousin." To say I was surprised was an understatement. Never once did it cross my mind that he would have been involved, but Wade Collins was standing just a few feet away with a Beretta pointed directly at us.

Fear surged through me when I heard a cry from outside the barn. I turned and started forward, but Leon appeared in the doorway with Aaron in his grasp. Leon held a gun loosely in his other hand. I could feel my temper rising, and my fists clenched at my sides.

"Take your hands off him," I growled. Leon laughed but didn't move. All at once, I felt a calmness settle over me. The knot in my stomach unraveled, and my breathing evened out. Turning to Wade, I said sharply, "Make him!"

"Now why would I do that?"

"Because if you don't, I won't cooperate." My voice was hard and cold. Wade would not have come here if he hadn't needed something. Something from me. "You want something."

"True," Wade said nonchalantly. He studied me a moment. "Very well. A show of good faith. Leon, let the boy go."

Out of the corner of my eye, I saw Leon release Aaron. The boy stumbled a couple of steps and then hurried over to us. Myra pulled him to her, and I stepped in front of both of them.

"So what do you want?"

"Rose's ruby ring."

What the hell did he want with that ring? "I don't have it with me. It's in a safe deposit box at the bank."

"I know. Which is why you're going to come with me to retrieve it while Leon stays here with his wife and the boy." I narrowed my eyes as he continued, "And just so everyone behaves, we'll keep the lines of communication open."

Wade raised one hand. In it, he held a cell phone. He dialed a number, and we heard Leon's phone ring. "We'll keep them on speaker."

"I need my purse," I said. I wasn't sure what to do. But until I knew neither Aaron nor Myra were going to be hurt, I was going along with Wade's plans.

"Why?" he asked, watching me.

"The safe deposit box key and my ID are in it. We can't get the ring without them."

He nodded once and gestured toward the door. I turned my back on him for just a minute and looked at Myra and Aaron. Anger surged through me, but I clamped it down. Myra's eyes met mine. I could see the resolve on her face. Her arm tightened around Aaron, and she nodded slightly. She would do everything in her power to protect him. My heart broke when I glanced at Aaron. He was trembling and swallowed once, but he raised his chin and glared at Wade. I quickly blinked away tears before walking out of the barn.

The walk to the front of the house was conducted in silence. My fear returned the farther away from Aaron and Myra I went. Wade followed closely behind me. I quickly opened the door and grabbed my purse from the small table by the door. I could hear Harry making his way from the back of the house. We had shut Harry inside. When he was around the horses, he got very excited and made them skittish. Quickly, I closed the door softly behind me, but didn't hear it click.

"You drive," Wade said, pointing at a gray sedan.

I walked over to the driver's side and got in. Thinking frantically, I tried to come up with a plan. Wade was not going to let any of us live once he had the ring. I needed to decide how to stop him before we got to that point. Having my purse with me helped settle my nerves some. Wade didn't know I had my Glock stashed inside. Unless he had done some extensive research on me before coming to town, he didn't know about my shooting expertise. It was one advantage I hoped to use.

We drove down the short drive and headed into town. Wade pulled on a cheap rain jacket and put on a canvas hat. No wonder the man I saw leaving the library after meeting with Ricky seemed familiar. It wasn't much of a disguise, but it would fool most people. No one was looking for Wade Collins. We all thought he had gone back to New York. As we got closer to town, he spoke with Leon.

"I want to hear Myra and Aaron's voices," I said.

"You really aren't in any position to make demands," Wade said softly.

I slowed the car down. "I'm not going any farther until I know they're both safe."

Wade sighed dramatically. "Very well. Leon."

"We're here, Leah," Myra said. I heard her whisper something, and a moment later Aaron's voice came through the speaker. I released a breath I didn't even know I had been holding. Wade adjusted his hat and pulled up his collar. I drove at a sedate pace, buying time, but it didn't take us long to reach Main Street. I turned right and took a deep breath.

"Why the ring?" I asked. "It's not worth that much."

"The ring is the key," Wade said. I glanced at him, unsure about what he meant. "It unlocks the rose."

"The rose? The wooden rose Albert carved?"

"Yes," Wade replied. He settled back in the seat. The Beretta rested on his lap, and he held it absently. Maybe I could use the car speed to jar it out of his hand. I started to speed up and then remembered Leon would hear anything I did. I needed to get him off the phone before I could act.

"You still haven't figured it out, have you?" Wade continued. "All this time you had access to millions but didn't even know it."

"Why don't you explain it then?" I was getting a little pissed at his condescending attitude.

"Sure, why not?" Wade chuckled softly. "Arthur hid the missing gems inside the rose. When he and Albert were young and still close, they created a secret hiding place. Albert carved the rose with a hidden compartment. The bottom opens with the turn of the key."

"And the ruby ring is the key," I said. Things were finally beginning to make sense. "You killed Donnie for the ring?"

"He wouldn't give it to me," Wade said harshly. "If he had just given it to me, he could have lived. But he wouldn't. Said he discovered Arthur's secret and didn't plan to share so I broke the bastard's neck."

I swallowed once and tried to keep my voice even. Wade was one angry man. "I didn't realize you were in the military."

"That's because I didn't tell you. Didn't want anyone to know. One of the few things I learned from Uncle Sam was how to kill. It has come in handy a time or two over the years."

A shutter ran through me at the thought that Wade had obviously killed before. I didn't like my chances of surviving against him. I pulled to a stop at a light near downtown and looked around, hoping for an escape, but the streets were almost deserted. It was still too early for most of the shops to be open. In thirty minutes, the area would be busy. Unfortunately, that didn't help me now.

"I knew someone would recognize the technique sooner or later," he said before continuing so softly I almost didn't hear him. "I just didn't expect it to be so soon."

Griggs and Reddish thought the killer had military experience right from the start. Wade probably hadn't expected our police force to have that type of knowledge. Of course, other than Griggs and Reddish, it didn't. I pulled slowly through the light. We were almost at the bank, and I still didn't have a plan.

"You needed Jose to make a replica of the ring because Donnie hid his from you," I said.

There was silence in the car for a moment. I looked over at Wade and could see his jaw working. He was angry, but when he spoke, the tone was still smooth and casual. It was quite frightening.

"He had two made, actually. I found one. Just not the other. The police found…didn't matter anyway. The fake rings don't work. Jose was supposed to create one with the same ridges and curves as the original, but even he couldn't get it right."

Arthur and Albert had been master craftsmen. They created the perfect hiding place. I wasn't surprised the fake rings didn't open the rose. The design would have had to been perfect to fit.

"Why didn't you just break open the rose? Use a saw or something?"

"You think I didn't consider that?" Wade bit out. "I studied the designs. It was impossible to tell exactly where the compartment began and ended. The diamonds would have been fine, but the one gem that's worth half a million dollars is a fire opal. They are soft stones. Cutting into the rose without knowing where it was could have damaged it."

I didn't say anything else. We pulled into the bank parking lot. This was where Wade's plan was going to fall apart. There was no way Wade and I could walk into the bank and retrieve the ring without my having to introduce Wade to at least three people. He didn't know the people in Reed Hill. He didn't realize we would be stopped repeatedly to visit. He was used to the anonymity of New York City. I had to find a way to stop him before we went inside. I took a deep breath and turned to him.

"Now what?"

"Now, we go in and get the ring," he replied.

"If you leave the phone on, someone is going to hear something. The horses, feet shuffling, someone talking. They'll ask questions." I could hear Clover snorting and huffing through the speaker. It wasn't loud, but it was just enough to get someone's attention.

Wade looked at the phone and then back at me. I kept my face carefully blank. If I could just get him off the phone, I might have a chance. Wade gave me an evil smile.

"Leon, we're going into the bank now. I'm disconnecting us. If we aren't back on the line in twenty minutes, you know what to do."

Twenty minutes. I had twenty minutes to take down Wade and get back to Aaron and Myra. I picked up my purse and started to get out of the car. Wade grabbed my arm and squeezed it hard. I bit back a scream.

"Don't try anything," he said viciously. "Anything happens to me, your friend and the kid will pay the price."

I nodded. Wade slipped the gun into his pocket, and we got out. While he was walking around the car to me, I slipped my hand into my purse and pulled out the Glock. By the time Wade had rounded the sedan, I had it in my hand. I kept it hidden from him until he got close. Just as he stopped in front of me, I swung my purse up and across his face. He fell backward, stumbled briefly but regained his footing quickly. With a snarl, he jumped toward me. I fell back and landed on the ground. I looked up at him and saw his face grimace in fury. He pulled out the Beretta and pointed it at me. I twisted over just as he pulled the trigger. The bullet flew past my head. I heard screaming and shouting but didn't dare look away from the madman glaring down at me. Heart pounding, hands sweating, I raised my own gun. A shot went off. I watched as Wade's head snapped back, and he fell to the ground.

Chaos broke out after that. People swarmed around us. I stared at my hand, wondering how the gun had gone off. I was still staring at it when Griggs grabbed my arms and pulled me up. "Are you all right?"

I looked at him in shock and then over at Wade. Two police officers were on the ground next to him starting CPR. Megan was standing nearby, gun pointing at his still body and talking on the phone. I could hear sirens in the distance. My brain finally clicked in, and my eyes flew to Griggs.

"What?" he demanded.

"He has them," I whispered. "Leon has them. I have to go. I have twenty minutes."

"Leah, what are…"

I was already opening the door and sliding in. I quickly started the car and began to back out, shouting for everyone to get out of my way. Griggs ran around the car and jumped into the passenger's side. "Leah, wait, we need a plan."

"NO!" I screamed. "I'm not waiting. He has them. He has Aaron and a gun."

I knew I wasn't making any sense. I was barely coherent. Urgency ran through me. I had to get to them. Griggs asked me questions. I answered but have no memory of what I said. Whatever it was, it did the trick. Griggs got on his phone and cleared the way. We drove through town at a record speed. As we neared Myra's house, Griggs touched me lightly on the arm.

"We can't go rushing in there. If he sees you, he may start shooting. We need to find a back way in. Tell me everything you know about the layout."

Desperate, I nodded, took several deep breaths, and told him about the barn. We pulled to a stop in front of the house and made our way around it. The barn was toward the back of the property. I could see Maxie still in the paddock. Griggs motioned me to stay and started around back. I couldn't stay still and headed across the lawn.

A bark sounded through the air, and I gasped as Harry came running from the barn. I took several steps closer, trying to calm him down and hoping Griggs had made it around back. The door of the barn slowly opened. I froze. Myra stood just inside the doorway. She looked around and then back at me.

"Where's Wade?" she called.

"Down," I said.

It was all I could think of to say. Myra sagged in relief. Shaking, I took another step toward her. I could feel the tears filling my eyes. Myra reached behind her and pulled Aaron forward. The tears spilled over, streaming down my face, as I fell to my knees. Aaron took two steps forward and then broke into a run. He barreled into me, and I gathered him close. I don't know how long we sat there before he finally started to squirm. I slowly let him go. He placed his two hands on my shoulders and looked me in the eye.

"Harry jumped on Leon, and Myra hit him in the back of the head with a pitchfork." He gave me a huge grin. "It was

AWESOME."

CHAPTER 24

Three days later, I was standing next to Daniel Thompson as they laid Jose Alvera to rest. Daniel had asked me to accompany him to the services. The old man didn't have very many friends, and Jose's death had hit him hard. I had been worried about him for a while, but he seemed to be back to his usual grumpy self.

Wade had died on the way to the hospital. I hadn't killed him. I had not even pulled the trigger. Everything happened so quickly that I couldn't remember even raising the gun, but it turned out that Megan had shot him. Secretly, I'm glad. I would have done whatever I needed to save Aaron and Myra but killing Wade would have weighed heavily on me. I'm sure it weighed heavily on Megan too.

The police presence had been a surprise to me. At the time, I didn't think they knew anything about Wade, but Ricky had finally spilled all. Griggs and the others spanned out in search of Wade. When one of them reported seeing me driving into town in an unfamiliar car, they had convened quickly. Once Wade pulled his gun, Megan had acted.

Between Ricky and the items we found in Wade's hotel room, the whole sad story came out. Wade, like his great-grandfather, had gotten involved with the criminal underworld.

Unlike Albert, Wade did not pay his debts. He owed a great deal of money to some very nasty people. When he learned of Donnie's plan, he saw an easy way out.

When he was cleaning out his grandfather's house, Donnie had discovered not only Rose's letter and Arthur's sketches, but Albert's designs as well. Donnie was even smarter than Wade had let on. He did a little digging and learned about the missing gems and the hidden compartment. A little more research revealed that my grandmother, Sadie—Rose and Arthur's daughter—had left both the rose and the ring to me.

The original plan was simple and even a little elegant. With Donnie's connections, he was able to find someone to design the fake rings, but he didn't have anyone to create the rose. That is where Ricky came in. He got Sean to carve the rose in exchange for the Vicodin that Sean needed. Sean isn't much of a sculptor on his own, but he is good at recreating other's designs.

Donnie's plan was to break into my apartment, replace the real rose with the fake one, and disappear. No one would ever know about the theft, and no one would get hurt. Wade changed all that. He was frightened and desperate. When Donnie went to the park to get the fake rose from Sean, not to meet me as I originally thought, Wade killed him, took the rose and his shoes, knowing the ring was probably hidden in the heel. One of them had been, but Wade still needed the original rose. He stopped by the store to meet me, and I fell right into his plans. One look at Albert's rose, Wade knew the fake one would never pass as the original so he hired Leon to steal it.

"So Wade killed both Donnie and Jose?" Daniel asked as we walked back to the car. Between the funeral and the graveside service, I had filled him in.

"Yes. The rings that Ricky had made didn't open the rose's hidden compartment. He needed Jose to create another one. Jose tried but he wasn't able to recreate a stone with the exact cut as the real one."

"That boy should've stayed out of it," Daniel said grumpily.

"He needed the money to pay for his brother to go to

medical school."

Daniel grunted but didn't say a word. Jose's part in the plan was the saddest. He just wanted to help his family. He knew he was in too deep but didn't know how to get out. Ricky put a lot of pressure on him because of Vanessa. After Donnie was murdered, Ricky was approached by Wade. At first, he refused to help. He really was trying to go straight. Working with Donnie was supposed to be his last illegal job, a way to help a friend and earn a little extra money. Once Vanessa disappeared, Ricky didn't know what to do. He had planned to marry the girl. Wade threatened him with her. Luckily, we found her scared but alive in a room at the Main Street Inn.

"Are you sorry you're not rich?" Daniel asked me as we pulled into my parking spot behind Scents and Sensibility.

"No," I said with a sigh. "I just wish no one had died. I would have given the rose to Wade or Donnie if they had just asked."

The rose had been empty. I had gotten the ring out of the safe deposit box and found the hidden compartment, but the gems were long gone. If they were ever there. Donnie, Jose, and Wade had died for nothing.

"Sounds to me like your cousins never thought of that. Wade and Donnie weren't the type of people who would just hand over millions."

"I doubt the stones would have been worth that much. For some reason, Wade and Donnie were convinced that the fire opal was worth close to half a million dollars. They were wrong. I did some research. They never could have sold it for that much."

"They were past rational thought," Daniel said. "All wrapped up in the history. Stupid boys."

Daniel stomped off. I watched him walk over to his store's back door and go in. Sighing softly, I knew Daniel was right. There was nothing Wade wouldn't have done to get those stones. He was convinced they would save him.

Emma was sitting at the desk when I opened the back door to Scents and Sensibility. She had returned from her vacation rested, relaxed, and full of questions about everything that had happened while she was gone. Myra and I had taken turns filling her in before I left for the funeral.

"How was the service?" she asked when I sat in the chair opposite her.

"Fine. Nice. Sad. All the things a funeral should be."

"How's Daniel doing?"

"Okay," I replied. "I think he's going to be all right. It just makes me wish I had gotten to know Jose better. Daniel's very selective about his friends."

"What's going to happen to Ricky and Leon?"

Leon had to be treated for a concussion. Myra had hit him pretty hard. After I had left with Wade, Harry managed to get the front door of the house open. I hadn't pulled it completely shut behind me. I'm still not sure if I had done that consciously or not. Many aspects of that morning remain a blur. I was operating on pure adrenaline and fear.

It had taken Harry some time to get out, but he made his way to the barn. Leon already had a healthy fear of the dog after Harry attacked him in my apartment. He would have shot Harry if he hadn't been distracted. According to Aaron, the dog raced in and jumped on Leon, causing him to lose his grip on the gun. Myra grabbed the nearest weapon, which just happened to be a pitchfork, and hit him in the back of the head. Leon went down without a fight. She then tied his hands and feet with some horse leads. They probably wouldn't have held him long, but Leon was just coming around when Griggs and I arrived.

"Leon will be going to prison for a long time. He didn't murder anyone, but he was an accessory. He also kidnapped Aaron and Myra and held them at gunpoint."

"And all he has to show for it is a concussion," Emma said dryly.

We both laughed. The blow to Leon's head had years of anger and frustration behind it. Leon had been mostly incoherent when they loaded him into the ambulance. Gabe, Olivia, and I were worried that Aaron might have to testify at his trial. Aaron seemed to have weathered the ordeal fairly well, but his parents were keeping a close eye on him.

As soon as he was lucid, Leon had lawyered up. We still didn't know how he and Wade had gotten together. Had they known each other in the past? Or was Leon just someone Wade managed to lure into his plans with promises of riches? Leon wasn't talking so we might never know.

"And Ricky?"

"Well, Ricky's a different story," I said slowly. "Technically, he didn't commit any crime except for obtaining the Vicodin for Sean. And the police can't prove that. They could charge him with conspiracy to commit a crime, and maybe as an accessory to murder, but considering he was being blackmailed with his girlfriend's life, I doubt he'll face any serious charges. He's on probation so he might have to spend a little time in jail."

"I'm just glad everyone is safe." Emma rose from the chair. "Are you staying?"

It was my day off, but I had come in to update Emma and pick up Daniel for the funeral. "No, I'll be leaving in a few minutes."

She nodded and left me with my thoughts. They weren't happy ones. My distant relatives had brought a lot of heartache to my town. It bothered me, probably more than it should have. A knock on the back door pulled me from my chair. Griggs stood on the other side with a small box in his arms.

"Hi," he said as I stepped back to let him in.

"Hi."

I hadn't seen him since Saturday when I had given my statement to Megan. The day had been hectic and felt unending. Olivia had closed the store the minute I called her. She and Gabe had rushed out to Myra's. Olivia took Aaron home while Gabe came to the police station with me. It took hours to get everyone's story. Griggs had spoken to me once but had little time to spare.

"How are you?" he asked as he sat the box on my desk.

"Fine. You?" I was a master of small talk. I shook my head

and offered him a seat. We sat side by side silently for a moment.

"So I have…"

"What's in th…"

We spoke at the same time and then laughed at ourselves. He gestured for me to go first.

"What's in the box?" I asked.

Instead of answering, he leaned forward and opened it. "I spoke with Wade's father, Russell."

He then picked up the box and put it on my lap. I looked inside and saw the fake rose, a couple of sketchbooks, and a folder. I pulled out one of the sketchbooks.

"I asked him if he wanted me to return the sketchbooks and designs," Griggs continued. "He said no. I thought you might want them."

Arthur's jewelry sketches were beautiful. My family would cherish them. I personally loved Albert's designs but was surprised Russell didn't want them. When I said as much to Griggs, he just smiled sadly. "I don't think he wants the reminder."

I flipped through the books a moment. The books would be a wonderful heirloom, but I had no idea what to do with the fake rose. I pulled it out and studied it. It was actually pretty. Sean had done a good job. Compared to all the other items I had seen him create, the rose was a masterpiece. Of course, it would never replace the real one. Albert had been a genius when it came to wood carving. I placed the rose on the desk.

"It'll make a nice paperweight."

Griggs laughed softly and leaned back in the chair. He was dressed casually in jeans and a deep green polo shirt that brought out his eyes. I swallowed quickly as my mind went places it shouldn't. He just watched me with a knowing smile. I cleared my throat and asked, "What's happening with Ricky?"

There was a short pause before he answered. I could still hear the smile in his voice when he spoke. "He's out on bail. The DA is looking at the possible charges. I think he'll probably get a slap on the wrist. A year or so added to his probation."

"Are you okay with that?" I knew Griggs didn't think much of the Cantonos.

"He did come clean in the end," he answered with a shrug. "If he hadn't told us that Wade was involved and what he wanted, we wouldn't have known to look for you. Ricky was really worried about Vanessa. He should have come clean in the first place, but I get why he didn't."

Suddenly, he slapped his legs and stood. "Isn't today your day off?"

"Yes," I said as I rose. "I was just about to head home."

"How about we grab something to eat and go bowling?" He reached over and took the box from me and started for the door. I stared at him in shock.

"Bowling?" I squeaked as I followed him out the door.

He grinned as he placed the box in the trunk of my car before leading me to his SUV. He opened the door, and I got in. He leaned forward to look me in the eye. I caught my breath and felt my heartbeat speed up. He smiled slowly before kissing me softly on the lips.

"It's the only place I can think of that you won't find someone to follow or question. Maybe we can actually get to the end of the date this time."

A huge smile crossed my face, and a feeling of anticipation ran through me. Griggs rounded the car and got in the driver's side. He looked at me questioningly. His own grin answered mine. I tilted my head and said, "I don't know why you want to take all the fun out of it."

"Tell you what," he said mischievously. "During dinner, you can question me and afterwards, you can follow me. All the way back to my place."

###

ABOUT THE AUTHOR

B. L. Blair writes simple and sweet romance and mystery/romance stories. Like most authors, she has been writing most of her life and has dozens of books started. She just needs the time to finish them.

She is the author of the Holton Romance Series and the Leah Norwood Mysteries. She loves reading books, writing books, and traveling wherever and as often as time and money allows. She is currently working on her latest book set in Texas, where she lives with her family.

Other titles by B. L. Blair:

Convince Me (Holton Series #1)
Notice Me (Holton Series #2)
Trust Me (Holton Series #3)
Forgive Me (Holton Series #4)

Dead in a Dumpster: Leah Norwood Mystery #1

Connect with B. L. Blair online:
http://www.blblair.com
https://twitter.com/blblair100
https://www.facebook.com/blblair100